I Spy

Joan Peake

First impression – 2004

ISBN 1 84323 332 0

© Joan Peake

Joan Peake has asserted her right under the Copyright,
Designs and Patents Act, 1988, to be identified
as Author of this Work.

This book is published with the financial support of the
Welsh Books Council.

Printed in Wales at
Gomer Press, Llandysul, Ceredigion SA44 4JL

*To Ann
with thanks for all the hard work
and support*

Chapter 1

I'm late for school, Myra thought, and it's all those beastly Germans' fault. The siren had sounded again last night, just after they'd gone to bed and Mam had made them go down the shelter at the bottom of the garden – just as she'd been getting cosy and warm.

They'd all protested. 'Aw, Ma-am! Do we have to? There haven't been any bombs dropped on Cardiff for ages.'

But Mam had insisted and they'd been down there for hours in the cold and damp. Why couldn't they have bunk beds like the ones Mr Davis up the street made. But Dad was no good at carpentry and all they had were some old dining-chairs with mock leather seats. Her back still ached after sitting bolt upright for hours and the rexine covers were so cold and hard her bum went numb after a bit. And it was impossible to sleep anyway with the pom-pom-pom of the guns going off on Penylan Hill and the drone of the planes overhead. They'd probably been on their way to Swansea or Port Talbot – anyway, it hadn't been Cardiff's turn last night.

And Gillian got on her nerves, too, fussing about spiders all the time. And who cared if she hadn't had time to put her Dinky curlers in? If you were dead no one would worry if you didn't look like Betty Grable!

Still, Mam did her best, fair play. Myra licked her lips

at the memory of the hot cocoa and Marmite and tomato sandwiches that her mother always made when they came up after the all-clear sounded – though the cocoa didn't warm them up for long. Last night she'd been so cold, she couldn't get to sleep. After tossing and turning for ages, she'd crept downstairs and taken the shelf out of the oven at the side of the still-hot fire, wrapped it in a towel and put it in her bed to warm it. She had fallen asleep in the end, but they'd all found it hard to wake up this morning.

Gillian was late for work. She'd hastily swallowed a cup of tea, but when Mam said, 'Wait and have a piece of toast,' Gillian had grabbed her handbag saying, 'Can't stop. I'll have a couple of biscuits in the shop,' and run. She worked in Liptons, the grocers, so she could help herself from the row of glass-topped containers. They'd keep her going until lunch-time. Lucky dab, Myra thought, enviously.

Mam said, 'Come on. Hurry up! You're late already. I'll just put some jam 'n marg on this bread and make you some sandwiches – you can eat them on the way to school.'

'Can't you move faster than that?' Myra shouted at her brother. Peter had another of his colds and he wheezed and puffed as he tried to keep up with her. 'I'm going to have a late mark. You'll have to get a move on when you go to the High School – that's if you pass, of course,' she added, nastily, taking her lack of sleep out on her brother.

'I can't walk as fast as you,' Peter complained. 'I get out of breath.'

'Well, I'm going on,' Myra said. 'I'll have to run if I'm going to get there before the bell goes.'

Leaving her brother at the turning for his school, Myra hurried through the Bowling Green lane. A sudden burst of gunfire from her right made her jump. Bullets whined and ricocheted off the high wall where the army hung their targets in the field that backed on to the lane. One day, thought Myra, one of those bullets is going to bounce off the wall and hit me in the eye and I'll have to have a glass eye like Dad's Cousin Lizzie.

As she scurried on her way, she saw a man standing quite still among the bushes further along at the side of the path. He seemed to be staring through the high fence that guarded the barracks field.

What's he doing there? Myra wondered. Funny place to have a pee . . . all the people will be able to see him from the barracks side. She slowed down, nervous about passing him. What had Mam said about walking this way on her own? But perhaps if she just crept by quietly, and didn't look at him, he wouldn't notice her.

The man heard her coming. He wheeled round at the sound of her footsteps, the sun glinting on his steel-rimmed spectacles. For a moment, he reminded her of how Peter looked when he'd been caught out doing something wrong. Then his face changed – and he smiled at her, though she couldn't see his eyes through the thick lenses.

'I think I might have lost my keys somewhere along here last night,' he said. 'I've looked everywhere, but no luck, I'm afraid. I don't suppose you've seen them, have you?'

Myra shook her head as he stumbled towards her through the brambles. How could he have possibly dropped his keys over by the fence? What had he been doing in the lane last night, anyway? No one ever came this way when it was dark.

'I came this morning to see if I could find them. If you see them . . .' As he put his hand in the pocket of his long black overcoat, Myra swallowed. Did he have a gun? Visions of herself lying in a pool of blood with her mother and Gillian sobbing above her flashed through her mind as she backed away – but when the man took his hand out, all he had in it was a handkerchief. He polished his glasses and stuffed the hanky back in his pocket. Then, as he withdrew his hand, a small white card fluttered to the ground. With a stiff little bow he turned to go. It was only then that she noticed he limped badly. He was like that wooden puppet that Peter used to have, all jerky and stiff, she thought to herself. Should she tell him he'd dropped something . . . ? No, better not call him back.

When he'd disappeared through the gate at the end of the path, she picked up the card. 'The Flottmann Drill Company, Allensbank Road, Cardiff,' she read. Now where had she heard that name before? She shoved the card into her coat pocket. Crumbs, she was going to be really late if she didn't get a move on.

She sprinted past the gates of the boys' school and on down New Zealand Road. Dashing into the girls' school entrance, she hung up her coat and hat, buttoned the straps of her indoor shoes and hurried to her form room. Everyone had gone to assembly. She slung her satchel and gas mask under her desk and raced along the corridor to the hall, skidding on the gleaming block floors.

Hope I don't see any prefects, she thought. I can do without lines for running in the corridor.

'Fight the good fight', sang the girls in the hall. Gosh, the first hymn already! She was just about to slip through the double doors, when a cold voice said, 'Myra Weaver, you are very late. Come to my office after prayers. I'll hear your explanations then.'

Her heart sank. It was Miss Richards, the Headmistress. She hadn't heard her coming in those rubber-soled shoes she always wore. Sneaky old thing, thought Myra, always scuttling along with her head poking forward as if she couldn't wait to get wherever she was going. And that awful droopy tortoise-coloured skirt!

Resignedly, Myra held the door open for Miss Richards and followed her into the hall.

'What . . . happened . . . to . . . you?' sang Abigail, to the tune of 'Fight the good fight' as Myra joined her and Margaret, her two best friends, at the end of their form's row.

'Tell you later,' Myra hissed.

After prayers she told her form mistress, Miss Jones, that Miss Richards wanted to see her in her room.

'Very well, but come straight back here afterwards. It's English first period.'

Myra knocked on the secretary's door and was told to wait while she checked to see if the Headmistress was free.

11

'Yes, Miss Richards will see you now,' she said.

Myra tapped on the door, her knees trembling.

A stern voice said, 'Come!' and when Myra appeared around the door, Miss Richards said, 'Ah, yes. You were late – and not only late, you were running in the corridor. Now you know that it is expressly forbidden because it can lead to accidents. Take a hundred lines to be handed in tomorrow. "I must walk along the passageways in school". And may I ask why you were late?'

Myra stammered, 'It was the raid. We had to go down the shelter – and I couldn't sleep afterwards – I was so cold. Then I overslept.'

Miss Richards' voice was softer as she asked, 'Don't you have an alarm clock?'

'Dad usually calls us at half-past seven when he goes to work but I couldn't have heard him.'

'Well, this time we'll forget about the late mark. But remember, in future, walk in the corridors.'

'Yes, Miss Richards.'

Relieved, Myra left the room. She nearly broke into a run down the long passageway, but remembered in time and walked sedately back to her form room.

'Ah, Myra. We're reading Act Two, Scene One, *Julius Caesar*. Brutus's speech. Right Abigail, carry on.'

Myra found the place and listened as Abigail stumbled through the speech, thinking how lucky she'd been to escape a late mark. But it would take ages tonight to copy out all those lines.

At break-time, Abigail said, 'What were you going to tell me? Did you have an incendiary through the roof or something?'

12

'No. It was just – something happened on the way to school.' She went on to tell Abigail about the man.

'He was really scary. He was dressed all in black and he had horrible steel-rimmed glasses and he had something wrong with his leg. He limped along like a grasshopper. Like this, look!' Myra showed how he walked. 'I think he's a German spy. You know how all those posters warn you about looking out for suspicious characters.'

Abigail gave her one of her looks, 'Go on, don't be so daft . . . Just because you see one funny looking man . . .'

'No, honest.' Myra searched in her pocket for the card. 'Look at this – he dropped it in the lane. See the address? Isn't that the place where that spy used to work? You know – the one that scarpered just before war broke out?'

'But this man you saw could just be working there,' scoffed Abigail.

'Why would he be over by the railings at night, then? I think it was just an excuse, losing his keys. I bet he was watching the soldiers – seeing what guns they've got and stuff like that,' argued Myra stubbornly.

'You've been listening to the wireless too much. Or was it that film you saw on Saturday morning? My Mum always says you've got too much imagination.'

Myra was cross. Fancy Mrs Pryce talking about her like that. Did she think she told lies? She decided not to tell Abigail any more, not if she wasn't going to believe her.

'Anyway,' Abigail went on. 'What did Miss Richards say to you 'cos you were late?'

'Got lines – and asked me if I had an alarm clock. That means I probably won't have time to read my book tonight. It's great! *Madcap of the Fourth*. They're making a school magazine. I wish we could do that.'

'What would we put in it?'

'Oh,' Myra waved her hand vaguely. 'Stories and that. I could make up a spy story about that man.'

'Oh, you and your stories.'

Myra said, huffily. 'Oh, all right. If you're not interested, I'll see if Margaret or Dorothy will have a go.'

'I didn't say I wouldn't. But what would I write about?'

'Anything. Jokes. A poem. Whatever you like.'

'Oh, yeah. I can see me writing poetry, can you?'

'Well, try.' Myra dredged up one of her mother's sayings. 'You don't know what you can do until you try.'

As she walked home from school that evening, she heard someone call her name. It was Denis, one of the gang she hung around with in her street.

He fell into step with her and, as they passed the Barracks field, Myra told him about the man she'd seen that morning. 'I told Abigail about him, but she more or less said I was imagining things.'

Denis whistled. 'Sounds suspicious to me. We better tell Eddie and the others. You know where he works, we'll follow him and see what he's up to.'

'Good idea! I'll call for Joyce and Bernadette on the way home and tell them. You call for Eddie, will you? I know he only lives next door, but what's-his-name might come to the door and I don't fancy him. I don't know why.'

'Who? Old Slater? Eddie's lodger! Oh, he's okay,' Denis said. 'Last Saturday he gave me and Eddie money to go to the tuppenny-rush. Anyway, see you in half an hour – that's if the siren doesn't go.'

Chapter 2

The gang met on the corner by the 'dead wall'. Myra wondered, not for the first time, why people called it that and the only reason she could think of was that there were no windows or doors in it. It was a good place to meet. In summer the boys drew stumps on the yellow brickwork and played cricket – until Mrs Edwards came out and shouted at them to 'Go away and play outside your own front!' A gas lamp lit the corner when it was getting dark and if they wanted a swing, they threw a rope over one of the 'arms'.

Bernadette was last to arrive. She'd had to look after her baby brother while Mrs McCarthy went to Mass at St Joseph's.

'What's up?' she asked. 'I can't stay long. I promised my mother I wouldn't be a minute.'

Denis looked at Myra. 'You'd better tell them. You were the one to see him.'

Myra drew herself up importantly, cleared her throat, and told the other four about the man in the lane.

'He said he was looking for his keys, but he wasn't looking down at the ground when I saw him. He was staring through the fence into the barracks.'

'What did it say on the card?' Eddie asked.

Myra took it out of her gymslip pocket. 'Here it is. You can see for yourself.'

Eddie was nearly fourteen, a year older than the rest of them. He always reminded Myra of Mrs Batchelor's golden Labrador, he was so big and friendly, while Denis was small and wiry and a bit of a nosey-parker like Paddy, her Nan's fox terrier. Eddie tended to take charge when they were all together, but Denis was the clever one they turned to when there was a problem.

Eddie looked closely at the card. 'Hmm. Allensbank Road. I suppose he could have been walking that way and dropped those keys.'

'He wouldn't have dropped them over by the fence,' Denis pointed out. 'It's nowhere near the path. Unless he did it deliberately, of course.'

'No, I suppose so,' agreed Eddie. Then, looking at the card again he said, 'Hey! d'you see the name of the company? Flottmanns! That's where that German spy worked.' His eyes blazed. 'He was the one who was taking photographs of the docks. He was the one who got my Dad killed.'

Myra remembered that afternoon. The siren had wailed while they were in school and all the girls had run across the playground towards the row of brick-built shelters that stood in a line against the fence on the far side. They could see this plane looking like a toy against the clear blue sky and thought it was one of theirs. They watched small objects falling diagonally from it. The giggling girls, who had at first thought this was just a false alarm and a good excuse for missing lessons, had started shouting and screaming, 'It's a Jerry!' Then they heard distant explosions that made the seagulls rise screaming and shouting from the rubbish tip at the

Maindy pool across the way and the teachers had shouted, 'Quick, into the shelters!'

Mrs Goodwin, Eddie's mother, had collapsed with grief and horror when the news had been broken to her and Eddie had called over the back wall to ask Mrs Weaver, Myra's mother, to come and help him with her. Myra's mother had run next door and made hot sweet tea, and sat trying to console her until her sister arrived.

Myra had heard the bad news on her way home from school. A neighbour told her, 'All six of 'em, blown to pieces, poor lads.'

'Blown to pieces!' Myra had been so shocked, she'd burst into tears and run home. When her mother eventually managed to get the story out of her through her sobs, she had been really angry.

'That Mrs Evans! No kids of her own! She should never have told you. I'll tell her, I will!'

She'd marched up the road to Mrs Evans's house and demanded, 'Did you have to tell my daughter about those men being killed in such a callous way? She's breaking her heart down there. You should have had more common sense.'

Mrs Evans had come to see Myra and apologised, saying, 'Sorry, love. Didn't mean to upset you. It just came out like that. I was upset myself.'

It was after that they'd heard about the German spy who used to live in Cardiff. He'd spent much of his time taking photographs from the small aircraft that ran pleasure trips to Weston-super-Mare. He'd made his escape by the skin of his teeth to Germany only a day or so before war broke out and Eddie was quite convinced that he was the person responsible for his father's death.

Eddie blinked hard. He took out a grubby handkerchief from his pocket and wiped his eyes, 'Must have got a bit of grit in my eye. It's gone now.' He looked around at them aggressively, 'Well, what we gonna do about him?'

'I bet he's another of 'em,' Denis said. 'Yeah! Let's get him.'

'You don't know that,' Bernadette said, quietly. 'You'll have to be careful.' Tiny, practical Bernadette was the eldest in a family of five and looking after her younger brothers and sisters had made her seem older than her years. Her grey-green eyes looked anxious now, peering from under the untidy fringe of auburn hair that had earned her the nickname of 'Carrots' at school. Denis impatiently swept her warning aside. 'Yes, but it looks suspicious. No one else would risk looking interested in the Barracks.'

Eddie brushed his sleeve across his eyes. 'Well, I'm going to watch him, see if I can catch him up to anything and if I do I'll get the police on him.' His chin set in a determined way. Myra knew that look – nothing would sway him.

Joyce said, 'Yeah, we can't let him get away with it. We could take it in turns to watch that place – there might even be a reward.'

Suddenly, the wail of the siren sounded and Myra's mother came to the front door.

'Come along,' she called. 'Down the shelter! And the rest of you run along home now.'

'It's probably a false alarm,' Myra said. 'You know they don't usually come over before dark.'

'This could be the exception. Now hurry. I just hope our Gillian has the sense to take cover.'

But almost before she'd jumped down into the shelter to join Peter, Myra heard the single note of the 'all clear' and began to scramble back out again.

When they were back in the kitchen, they saw their mother staring at a letter she'd received that morning.

'What's the matter, Mam?' Myra asked. 'Dad hasn't been called up, has he?'

'No, love. It's Peter.' She lapsed into silence again.

'What! I haven't been called up, have I?'

'Don't be daft,' said Myra. 'You're too young. You've got to be at least seventeen and a half.'

'It's from the Council. They want to evacuate you. The raids are getting worse and they want to send the youngest children away to a safer place. They may need to use the school for something else, see.'

'Well, I'm not going,' Myra said. 'If I went anywhere, it would be to Canada. A boy in our church went there, lucky dab. Fancy living on a ranch – just like the pictures – riding horses and that.'

Her mother gave her a funny look and sighed. 'Oh, I wish this war would end. When it started in 1939 they said it would all be over by Christmas. It's years now and still no sign of it ending. If anything, things are getting worse.'

'Where will I have to go, Mam?' Peter asked, anxiously. He was almost eleven and had never been away from home.

'Oh, not far, love. Probably out in the country. You'll be able to have farm eggs and fresh milk. Won't that be nice?'

Trust Mam to think of that, Myra thought. She was always fussing over Peter. He'd almost died of pneumonia just after he was born and he'd been in hospital twice since then.

'I wouldn't mind if we were all going. But I don't want to go on my own.'

'Other kids from your class will be going. And think of all the brave soldiers who have to go away from their families. They're not going somewhere nice out in the country, are they? They've got to fight. Think how lucky you are!'

But one look at Peter's crumpled face showed that he felt anything but lucky.

Just then they heard the front door close and their Dad came in. He worked long hours, starting at seven-thirty in the morning. Sometimes he didn't arrive home in time to see his children before they went to bed. He had a baker's round and delivered bread around the streets with his horse-drawn van. Star, his horse, knew the way so well that he remembered the houses where people gave him a sugar lump or a bit of bread. Myra had even seen him mount the pavement and stick his head in at the doorway until he got what he wanted.

Mam said Dad spent more time at the yard grooming Star and shining the brasses on his van than he did at home. Once a year he entered his outfit in the Horse Show at Sophia Gardens and then he would braid Star's mane and tail and twist ribbons in them, grooming him

21

until his coat shone like satin. His van was brushed free of crumbs and the brass lamps polished until you could see your face in them. He'd never won first prize, but he kept all the rosettes he'd won in a cupboard in the front room.

They heard Gillian's footsteps in the passage just then. She threw her gas mask case and handbag into an armchair and took off her coat.

'Look what he's given me to do – just 'cause I was late this morning!'

She held out a brown paper bag. 'Coupons! I've got to sort the ones for different foods into batches and count them. It's not fair.'

'Never mind, love. I'll give you a hand,' Mam said. Then turning to Dad, she said, 'Read this,' and handed him the letter from the Council.

He studied it for a moment, then pulled a face. 'You going to let him go?'

'We'll have to. It says it's for his own safety.'

'What about Myra?'

'I think it must be only for the younger ones. I was just telling them the Council may need the school buildings.'

Mam folded the letter, put it in the envelope and stuck it behind the clock on the mantelpiece.

'Nothing for me, was there?' Gillian asked. She had been writing to her boyfriend, Martin, a sailor she'd met in the Church Army canteen where she did voluntary work one evening a week.

'No, sorry, dear. Perhaps there'll be one tomorrow. You know he can only post letters when he gets to a port. You'll probably have two or three together soon.'

Gillian sighed. 'I'm so bored. I think I'll join up after my birthday.'

'You could go in the Land Army,' Myra said, mischievously, knowing that her big sister would hate to get her hands dirty.

'No, thank you!' Gillian retorted. 'I'll leave that to you.'

'Anyway, I'd better get tea in case the siren goes again tonight.'

'I've got to go out soon anyway,' said Dad. 'I'm on fire watch tonight. What are we having?'

'We'll have cheese on toast if you're in a hurry. It'll be the last of the ration, I'm afraid. Cut some bread, Myra and toast it in front of the fire. Don't get the black off the grate on it, will you?'

Soon they were sitting down to their meal. There was a hot bread pudding to follow that had been baking in the oven at the side of the fire most of the afternoon. It was Myra's favourite, even though there weren't as many currants in it as they used to have.

They listened to the news on the wireless as they ate and when they heard how the troops were faring overseas and about the towns that had been bombed, Myra's thoughts turned again to the man she'd seen in the lane. She was about to tell her mother and father about him, but Mam began a story of how she'd queued for sausages in the butcher's that morning.

'It was my turn to be served and then Mr Williams said, 'Sorry, that's the last.' I was so annoyed. I'd wasted all that time! I managed to get a couple of small hearts, but there wasn't time to cook them. They need doing slowly. We'll have them tomorrow. Oh, I was fed up. Still there's others worse off than us.'

Myra had just opened her mouth again, ready to tell her story about the spy, when the siren began to wail.

'Oh, not again. Can't they wait until we finish our tea?' Mrs Weaver piled the rest of the toast on to a plate and said, 'Come on, we'll have a picnic down the shelter. Bring a candle, will you, Myra? And don't forget the matches.'

'I'll cut along, love. Got to be on duty anyway.' Mr Weaver went into the passageway and took his coat, steel helmet and gas mask down from the peg.

Gillian said, 'I'll just run up and get my curlers.'

'Never mind your hair,' said her mother, but Gillian was already running upstairs.

Myra and Peter led the way to the shelter, but stopped outside the back door, for there, halfway down the path, flames spurted from something on the ground.

Peter crept forward cautiously to investigate, but Myra turned back and called to her father excitedly, 'Quick, quick, Dad! On the path – it's an incendiary, I think!'

Mr Weaver rushed out. 'Peter! Come back at once,' he yelled. 'It may be one of those exploding ones. I'll get the bucket.'

Quickly, he shovelled sand on to the small bomb, stifling the flames and, just to make sure, dug up some earth and piled that on top, too.

'Mind now, if you ever come across one of these when you're on your own, don't pour water on it. It would make it explode.'

He shepherded them to the shelter, making a wide detour round the incendiary in case it was still active.

'Get down the shelter now – and be good for your mother. I've got to go. Stay inside until the all-clear goes and keep the door in place until Mam and Gillian come. Night-night.'

Gillian came running down the path with her curlers and a small mirror in her hands.

'Come on, hurry up. Your life's more important than curls in your hair. Now stay under cover. Mam'll be down in a minute.' He put the wooden door back in place and they heard his footsteps retreating back up the path.

'Hurry up and light the candle,' said Gillian. 'I want to do my hair and inspect the place for slugs. Remember that horrible, slimy thing on the back of my chair? Ugh!'

Myra struck a match, lit the candle and placed it carefully in the holder on the cement ledge. She wondered how long they'd be down there tonight. The candle wouldn't last all that long.

It seemed ages before Mam came to join them, but just as the anti-aircraft guns began to sound, the door was lifted out of place and Mam climbed down into the shelter.

'Wherever have you been, Mam?' Gillian asked. 'Dad said you were coming down straight away. We were beginning to think something had happened to you.'

'I hadn't finished doing the blackouts. I was afraid one of you might go up afterwards and switch the light on. I still haven't finished them.'

The raid was a heavy one that night. Myra's tummy gave a lurch every time she heard the high-pitched scream of bombs as they hurtled to earth. Peter clapped his hands over his ears and Gillian pulled her cardigan over her head. Some were so close they could feel the earth tremble under their feet. Through the gaps in the shelter's ill-fitting door, Myra could see the flashing of searchlights as they trawled the sky for enemy bombers. The guns on Penylan Hill kept up that pom-pom-pom sound.

The noise was deafening. It was difficult to tell the difference between the row the guns made and the crash of bombs. Every so often a hail of incendiaries clattering like enormous hailstones on to roofs and pathways added to the din. The acrid smell of burning filtered into the shelter, keeping them on edge, listening in case the next scream would be the last thing they heard.

When it seemed to Myra that they had been there for ever, the all-clear sounded. They took down the door and climbed out into the night.

Yes, the house was still there, black against the flame-reddened sky. The smell of burning was stronger now, catching their throats and making them cough. Bits of shrapnel gritted under their feet as they scampered back up the path.

Peter strained his eyes to see if there were any large pieces of shell or bomb scattered around the garden.

'Don't you dare go picking up any of that stuff,' said Mam, from behind him. 'You know very well Dad's told you not to. Don't you remember hearing about that boy who had his hand blown off – he was lucky he wasn't killed.'

Reluctantly, Peter threw the small pieces of shrapnel he'd found back on the garden, Myra guessed he'd come back in the morning to retrieve them, though. There was keen competition in school amongst the boys to see who had the biggest collection and Myra knew that Peter had a shoebox full of bits and pieces he'd picked up after other raids.

As soon as they went indoors, her mother went upstairs to finish drawing the blackout curtains. She came down again carrying a rolled-up sheet in her hands and looking very annoyed.

'Part of the ceiling's come down on your bed, Gillian. There's plaster all over the place. You'll have to wait until I can clear it up. I'll just shake this on the garden. Put the kettle on, Myra, and you can make the sandwiches, Gill. Won't be a moment.'

She went out, muttering, 'That Hitler's got a lot to answer for. If I could get my hands on him, I'd give him what for!'

The girls exchanged glances and grinned at the thought of Mam giving Hitler a piece of her mind. She would, too, if she could.

As she filled the heavy iron kettle and lifted it over the fire, she wondered how Dad had fared in the raid. There seemed to be an awful lot of bombs dropped – and there were the incendiaries, too. It was part of his job as a firewatcher to put them out and now they had those exploding ones, it could be very dangerous. She tried not to think about the people who might have been killed or buried in their houses. She just hoped her father wouldn't be blown to bits like Mr Goodwin had been.

But the war came closer that night than she had ever known before. It was only when she went to school next day that she found out just how closely it had affected her, though.

Chapter 3

Denis was waiting on the corner of the street next morning. Peter grinned when he saw him, 'There's your boyfriend,' he said.

Myra turned on him. 'He's not my boyfriend. We've got something important to talk about, that's why he's waiting for me.'

'What? What's so important?'

'Never you mind. It's not for little kids like you.'

Peter pleaded, but Myra wouldn't tell him. Especially after he'd called Denis her boyfriend!

Denis and Myra talked about last night's raid, counting how many houses had had windows blown out by the blast, while Peter scanned the ground looking for pieces of shrapnel large enough to boast about to his friends when he arrived at school.

After he'd left them at the turning for Gladstone School, Myra and Denis could talk about the man she'd seen in the lane.

'Eddie and me had a chat about it last night and we think it'd be best if you came with us to that place where he works and point him out to us. We'd have to be under cover, so we thought we'd keep watch for him behind the cemetery wall. I know where my Dad's binoculars are, so we could use them.'

'Yeah, okay. Then we could take it in turns to watch him!'

'Don't think you should be in on it. He's seen you, it might be dangerous.'

Myra prickled. 'No more dangerous than it is for you. I suppose you think just because I'm a girl . . .'

'Well – he *has* seen you – and we don't want to put him on his guard. He might try to escape, like that other chap.'

Myra agreed reluctantly, then they parted to go in to their separate entrances.

There were little groups of girls in the playground waiting for the bell to ring. She saw Margaret and went over to her. Abigail must be late this morning, she thought.

'Heard the news?' Margaret looked anxiously at Myra.

'No, we didn't have the wireless on this morning. What?'

'Not that kind of news.' Margaret bit her lip. Her voice lowered. 'A bomb dropped on Abigail's house. A direct hit!'

'She's not . . . ?' A cold shiver ran through Myra and she stared dumbly at Margaret. Surely Abbie couldn't be dead! She sat next to her in class – and she didn't live far away; only off Albany Road.

'No, not Abigail – her mother. She left Abbie and her little sister in the shelter while she went to fetch something from the house.' Margaret looked around at the little group and nodded towards an older girl standing there. 'Grace lives in the next street. They had their windows blown out with the blast, but no one was hurt.'

'Thank goodness Abbie's all right,' Myra said. 'But her poor mother! Abbie must be feeling terrible! She and Amy will be all alone. Her father's in the Air Force; he won't be able to look after them.' Myra turned to Grace. 'Was Abbie hurt?'

'No, just shocked. A neighbour took them in, but I heard their Gran is coming from Tylorstown to take them back with her today.'

Tears pricked the back of Myra's eyes. Only yesterday she and Abbie had argued about that man. She wished she hadn't been so huffy with her. If she was going to stay with her Gran she might never come back to Cathays, so they wouldn't be able to make up. Abbie would probably have to live there until the war was over and her Dad came home. I'll miss her borrowing my ruler, asking me what I got for the answer to algebra problems, Myra thought. Abbie's Gran lived a long way away and Myra didn't even know her address.

A wave of anger swept over her. Those damned Germans! Why had this happened to Abbie? She'd never deliberately harmed anyone and now they'd killed her mother! If she proved that man was a spy, she'd make sure he couldn't send any more information to the enemy. She'd help the others track him down, get the truth out of him and hand him over to the police. She hoped they'd shoot him.

In the hall at prayers, without any of her usual briskness, Miss Richards told the school about Abigail's mother's death.

31

'I will be writing to Abigail extending our deepest sympathy on behalf of the staff and pupils . . . I know all of you, and especially her closest friends, will be feeling very sad as is only natural, but remember in times of war people receive bad news every day – and somehow they manage to carry on. To give in to emotion would be like giving in to the enemy. To undermine our confidence would be a great weapon for them – so we must fight it. I'm sure that is what Abigail would want you to do.

'Now, as a sign of respect, I would like you to bow your heads and keep silent for a moment.'

As they sang the last hymn, *Be Thou my Vision*, Myra couldn't help thinking how upset Abbie must be. She knew how she would feel if anything happened to Mam. A lump in her throat threatened to choke her and she felt the tears well into her eyes. She glanced up at Miss Richards to make sure she wasn't looking, then wiped her eyes with the sleeve of her blue blouse.

Once back in the classroom, Myra sat at her desk, very conscious of the empty seat next to her. Unbidden, tears rolled down her face. She fished in the pocket of her navy knickers for her handkerchief. But she'd lost it again. Lifting the lid of her desk, she hid behind it while she dashed away the tears, glad that she sat at the back of the room away from most prying eyes.

Everyone was subdued that day, with little enthusiasm for lessons, although their teachers did their best to interest them and take their minds off Abigail's sad news. Myra couldn't forget – not even for one minute.

As Myra turned the corner of the street on her way home that evening, she saw Joyce sitting on her bike outside Bernadette's house chatting to her. Joyce had passed the High School exam too, unlike Bernadette and Eddie, but she went to a different school from Myra and cycled because it was some distance away. Her dark brown hair was tousled, she'd tied her blazer over the handlebars of her bike. Her hat hung round her neck on its elastic and she'd taken off her tie and undone the top buttons of her blouse. Joyce didn't care about prefects.

Myra hurried along to join them. She had a lot to tell.

First she told them what had happened to Abigail's mother. 'It's been awful in school today with that empty seat next to me. I couldn't get her out of my mind. I wish I could do something to help her. I wonder if that man had anything to do with the bombing last night?'

Then she remembered what Denis had said on their way to school.

'I saw Denis this morning and he and Eddie have had an idea about that man – you know, the one I saw in the lane.'

As she told them what he'd suggested, she realised they'd have to move fast. While they were hanging about making plans, that man could be sending more and more information to the enemy.

'Oh, trust those two to want to do it all themselves,' said Joyce. 'What about us?'

'Perhaps they'll let you go with them,' Myra said.

'Don't you mind?' Bernadette asked. 'It was you who saw him in the first place.'

'Well, they thought if he saw me, he might realise we're on to him and clear out.' Myra shrugged. 'I suppose as long as we get him it doesn't matter who does it.'

'Well. I don't think it's fair and I'm going to tell them, too,' Joyce said.

A picture of Eddie sitting on his back door step came to Myra's mind. Her bedroom overlooked his back garden and she had seen him early this morning, his head in his hands – and he'd been crying.

She'd heard that George Slater shouting at him earlier and the sound of several slaps. Eddie must have done something to upset him again. She couldn't understand why his mother let that man Slater stay there.

'Don't say anything, Joyce,' Myra said, 'He's had a bad time lately what with his father being killed and everything. Looking for the spy may take his mind off it. Anyway, we're going up to that factory Saturday – see if we can spot him.'

But when Saturday came, Myra's mother kept her busy doing odd jobs and when she asked her to take a plate of dinner round to her grandfather's house so that her Dad could have a hot meal, it was the last straw.

'Aw, Ma-am. Can't Peter take it? I've been working all the morning and he's done nothing.'

'If I gave it to him he'd probably tip it or drop it. No, you must go. You're bigger than he is, anyway.'

She covered the hot dinner with another plate and then wrapped it in a clean tea towel to keep it warm, before placing it in the bottom of the large wicker basket she used for shopping.

'Can I go out with Joyce and the others when I come back?' Myra asked.

'Yes, I suppose so – as long as there's no raid.'

Myra hurried to her grandfather's house, the twisted

wicker of the basket's handle beginning to cut into her hand before she had gone very far.

Her father's two spinster sisters lived with Grampy. The older one, Auntie Pen, came to the door.

'Oh, what a nice surprise,' she said. 'Come in. What have you got there?'

Myra followed her through the long passageway and into the living room where the smell of Grampy's asthma cigarettes lingered in the air.

'Mam sent this dinner round for Dad so he could have something hot to eat.'

Auntie Kate took the basket from her. 'I'll put it over a saucepan of hot water,' she said.

Myra turned to go.

'Oh, you're not going already, are you?' Auntie Pen exclaimed. 'We haven't seen much of you lately. What have you been doing with yourself? How're you getting on in school?'

The thought of school made her think of Abbie again and she went on to tell them what had happened.

'Oh, that poor child! Of course, that street's not far from here. We were under the shelter – but the ground shook. I'm always afraid that the house will come down on top of us and we won't be able to get out.'

Grampy didn't have a shelter in the garden like theirs, he had a Morrison shelter in the living room – a sort of table affair with a steel top and strong steel mesh around the sides. They'd had to get rid of their small dining table to have this in its place. Myra often wondered how Grampy managed to crawl into it, what with his rheumatism as well as his asthma.

Just then, there was a knock at the front door and when Auntie Pen went to answer it, Myra heard her father's voice as he followed his sister back in.

'I could really do with a sit-down and something to eat,' he was saying. 'Saturday's a long day what with collecting the money and extra bread for the weekend. Hullo, love,' he greeted Myra. 'Thanks for bringing that round. Have you had your dinner?'

'No, I'd better go.' Myra made her escape. She'd still have time to meet Eddie and Denis if she hurried.

Eddie called over the back garden wall just as Myra was finishing her dinner.

'You ready?'

'Won't be a minute.' She turned to her mother. 'They're waiting for me. Can I go now?'

'I suppose so. Now don't be late.' She looked worried. 'Still no letter from Martin. Our Gill's going to be fretting. There's been nothing for weeks now. I hope nothing's happened to him. Still, sometimes they're at sea for ages before they dock.'

Myra hoped so, too. She liked Martin. He treated her as if she was his kid sister and always had a bar of chocolate or sweets for her and Peter. He looked really handsome too, in his bell-bottomed trousers and round sailor's hat.

Then she heard Eddie banging on the front door.

'That's them. I'm going now, okay?'

'Don't say okay,' her mother said automatically. 'And don't be late.'

'Okay.'

They called for Denis on the way and walked to the cemetery entrance in Fairoak Road, then cut across the grounds until they came to the gate in Allensbank Road where they had a good view of the factory, especially with Denis's binoculars.

They waited for ages, but the only people they saw were men in overalls crossing the yard. There was no sign of the tall man in a black overcoat and hat.

'He probably works in the office,' said Myra. 'He didn't look like a workman and he must have been wearing his ordinary clothes, because he would've been on his way to work at that time in the morning.

'Best thing we can do is to come here after school – he may not work on a Saturday,' said Eddie.

'We'll meet you after school Monday, then,' said Dennis.

'What about Bernadette and Joyce?' Myra asked.

'Yeah, they might as well come. If we see him they'll know who to look out for, then.'

But just as they were turning away, Myra gave one last look over her shoulder.

She grabbed Denis' arm. 'There he is! See? The one in the suit.'

She pointed to where a man was just emerging from the office building.

'There! Now you know who to look out for. He's easy to spot with those glasses and that limp!'

Chapter 4

There were quite a few girls from her form in the playground the following Monday at break and Myra thought it might be the ideal time to bring up the idea of a school magazine with them.

'Something like the one in that book I read, you know, *Madcap of the Fourth*,' she said. 'I did talk to Abbie, but of course she can't do it now.' She turned to Margaret. 'Will you write something? A poem, maybe?'

Margaret gasped. 'I can't write poetry!'

'Well, you can write something, can't you? Ask your mother for that recipe you said was nice. You know, the one with a tin of sardines that stretched for all the family.'

Margaret blushed. 'I wish I hadn't told you now.'

Dorothy, a pretty girl with cork-screw curls like Shirley Temple, said, 'I'll write something about the JACS if you like. I've just joined and it would be a way of getting more girls to come.'

Myra was immediately interested. 'What's the JACS?'

'Women's Junior Air Corps. We call it the JACS. It's not long started up in Allensbank School. It's great fun. We're learning how to send Morse code and do marching – everything. The ATC boys teach us.'

Allensbank School, thought Myra. That was quite close to where that spy worked. She'd have a good excuse for being there if the boys saw her – and she might be able to get some proof that he really was a spy.

Another thought occurred to her. It would be good training for when she was old enough to join one of the Forces, if the war wasn't over by then. She'd had a look at the posters recruiting nurses. That's what she wanted to do. She'd really liked being in the Red Cross and had good marks for bandaging and knowing the bones of the body. But when she passed the eleven-plus to come to Cathays High her mother had said there wasn't time for Red Cross – that her school work would suffer, so she had to leave. The same thing had happened with her piano lessons. But it was no good brooding about that now, there were other more important things to think about.

The only drawback was that you had to be seventeen before you could join any of the services and she was only thirteen. If she went to the WJAC she could be trained by the time she was old enough to join up, that's if the war went on that long – she might even be offered a commission!

'When d'you go?' she asked Dorothy. 'Can I come with you?'

'Yeah. 'Course you can. It's on a Friday night, seven o'clock, so it doesn't matter about homework.'

Not wanting Margaret to feel left out, Myra said, 'Want to come? It's only round the corner from your house.

Margaret pulled a face. 'No. I don't think so. I don't think my mother would let me go.'

'Why not? It would be helping the war effort.' She turned to Dorothy. 'Do you have to have a uniform?'

'Sort of. We haven't got it yet. They can't get the material. There's a shortage, see, because they need all they can get for the Airforce. But we're having forage caps – and they said if we've got a white blouse and grey skirt or something like that, we can wear them.'

'Mmm,' mused Myra, a uniform would be nice, but it was just as well it wasn't compulsory. If they'd had to give up coupons or pay a lot for uniform, Mam would say no.

'I'll ask my mother, but I don't think she'll mind. I'll let you know tomorrow.'

Her mother was busy sorting the washing when she broached the subject and Myra could tell she was only half listening.

'I'll be helping the war effort,' she said, earnestly. 'Can I?'

'Oh, I suppose so. You won't be late finishing, will you? I don't want you coming home at ten o'clock at night, what with the raids and all.'

'No, it ends at nine and I don't think they'd hold it if there was a raid on.'

Later, Myra asked Gillian if she would like to join with her.

'You're not too old and it would help when you went for your interview to join up. You could be an officer!'

'No thanks. Anyway, Martin might be home soon and I want to be able to see him as much as possible when he comes. We might be getting married on his next leave.'

'What?' Myra gasped. 'That's the first I've heard of it. When did he ask you? What'll Mam say?'

'What will Mam say about what?' Their mother's voice came from the back kitchen.

Both girls jumped.

'Gill says she might be getting married when Martin comes home. Can I be her bridesmaid?'

'I've never heard such nonsense. You're much too young. You can put that notion out of your head right now, young lady.'

'I'm nearly seventeen. You can get married at sixteen. Lots of girls are getting married now.'

'Not without your parents' consent – and you certainly won't have that. Not until you show more sense.'

'But we're engaged. Martin said on his last leave that if we both feel the same way about each other – he'll buy me a ring.'

'Well, he'd better come and see your father and me before he does. He might be wasting his money.'

Gillian stormed out of the room and up the stairs, banging her bedroom door behind her.

'Silly girl,' said her mother. 'She doesn't know what she's on about. Good heavens, she could be left a widow before she's twenty. God forbid, but it happens.'

Myra felt cold suddenly. She couldn't bear the thought of Martin lying wounded or gasping for breath as he fought the waves of the Atlantic – or blown to bits or burned to death. But it was true there hadn't been any letters for some time now. She hoped that it was just that he hadn't been able to post them.

Later, Myra called for Joyce to tell her about the WJAC, the Women's Junior Air Corps. 'I thought if we joined we could have a look at that factory where you-know-who works. The boys couldn't say anything about us being up there then.'

'Good idea. Shall we ask Bernadette?'

Bernadette came to the door carrying her baby brother Welsh-fashion, in a shawl wrapped around them both.

'Sorry – I can't come out. I've got to look after Patrick.'

'That's all right. We only want to ask you something.'

They told her about the WJAC. 'You see it's in Allensbank School, so I thought if we saw that man . . .'

'Yeah, well. That's all right for you, but my mother goes out on a Friday night and I have to look after the kids.'

'Can't she go another night?'

'No – she goes out with her friend. They always go on a Friday night. Sorry.'

Myra felt sorry for Bernadette. She missed out on a lot of fun. Myra thought it was mean of her mother to make her look after the baby so often.

'Never mind,' she said. 'We'll tell you what happens. And –' she brightened. 'Perhaps the boys will let you go with them. I'll have to stay home then.'

Bernadette smiled. 'Yes, I'll do that. Tell them to let me know when they're going.'

Myra found the front door ajar for her when she went home.

'Mam?' she called.

'Up here,' said her mother. 'I'm in Peter's bedroom.'

'What you doing?' Myra asked, seeing the open case on the bed and the piles of clothes her mother was sorting.

'They want Peter to go at the end of next week. I'm just trying to see what he should take with him. He could really do with some new things, but what with the coupons and everything . . . !'

She sighed. Myra knew she was thinking about the cost, too. Money was always tight. Every Friday night when Dad brought his wages home, Mam sat down with a piece of paper and a pencil and wrote down strings of figures trying to work out the best way to make the housekeeping go round.

'The thing is,' her mother went on, 'you know he's just sat the entrance exam for the High School. If he passes, it'll mean new school uniform and I'll need coupons for that I suppose. 'Still,' she brightened, 'perhaps Nanna will have a few to spare. She hardly ever buys anything new.'

'Will he come back if he passes?'

'I don't know. I'll have to find out. It depends on where they send him – whether there's a High School in the place.'

'I feel sorry for him really. He doesn't want to go. Now if he was going to Canada like that boy in our Sunday School did, I'd go with him.'

'Myra! Don't envy other people, you never know what trouble they might have.'

'Well, think of the fun we could have over there!'

'You realise you'd have to go on a ship, don't you?

And that there are U-boats in the Atlantic. The ship could be torpedoed. Look how many Merchant Navy ships have been lost.'

Myra was silent for a moment. Her mother always looked on the black side.

'I expect they'd put up a special flag or something to tell the U-boats there are children on board.'

Her mother gave an impatient shrug. 'I'll have to tell you. You won't take any notice otherwise. That ship the little boy from our church went on was sunk. Seventy-seven of those children were killed.'

She paused, seeing the look of horror on Myra's face.

'I didn't want to tell you, but you do keep on so. I'm amazed no one's told you already. It happened last September.'

Myra was stunned. All those little kids dying like Abbie's Mum. Everything seemed to be coming apart – like the jumpers that Nanna unravelled to make jerseys for Peter. How had that boy felt when he'd heard the bang and all the water rushing into the ship? Then the ship sliding lower and lower into the water – and the water closing over his head . . . Did he try to swim? Could he swim? Oh, why hadn't anyone told her about this before?

'I didn't know,' Myra muttered. 'Why didn't someone tell me?'

'I expect they didn't want to upset you – or perhaps they thought you already knew.'

'It's awful. Did everyone drown?'

'They *did* find a lifeboat or something about a week or so afterwards with some people in it – but not many.

Don't upset yourself now. Let's put the kettle on and have a nice cup of tea, shall we?'

Myra filled the big iron kettle and placed it over the fire. She had a cold feeling inside after hearing about Michael. That's another thing she had against that man she'd caught spying – but he'd get what was coming to him one of these days – she'd make sure of that.

Chapter 5

Myra and Joyce met Dorothy outside Allensbank School that Friday. Myra had brushed her light brown hair until it gleamed and she'd polished her shoes until they shone too – although she couldn't see her face in them as Dad said she should be able to. Her blue eyes sparkled in anticipation of the evening ahead. Myra's youngest aunt had given her a white cotton blouse that was too small for her and with it she wore a navy skirt made out of an old gymslip she'd torn climbing trees in the Heath Woods.

She was getting quite good at making do and mending. Everyone did it now. The *Echo* had a column that gave handy hints on how to recycle your old clothes. There'd been a good one recently that explained how to make a skirt out of the legs of a pair of men's trousers. Mam had made several pairs of short pants for Peter out of Dad's old ones.

As they entered the school they saw two officers dressed in air-force blue, chatting together in the lobby. Dorothy pointed to the one facing them.

'That's the officer in charge of the Air Training Corps boys,' she whispered.

Myra saw an older man with slightly greying hair who looked a bit like Douglas Fairbanks, her mother's favourite film star. He was listening intently to the other officer, a pleasant smile on his face.

The other man had his back to them, but hearing their footsteps, he turned. Myra's heart flipped over as she saw his steel-rimmed glasses. It was the spy! But what was he doing here – and in Air Force uniform?

His eyes narrowed when he saw Myra. 'I believe we've met before?'

Myra's mind was in a whirl. He'd recognised her!

'Ye-es,' she stammered. 'Did you find your keys?' She felt Joyce stiffen at her side.

'Thank you, yes. They were in my pocket at home after all.'

Myra forced a smile. 'Good.' She couldn't think of anything else to say.

The grey-haired officer said, 'You want the JACs, do you?'

Dorothy said, 'Yes. Are we in the usual room?'

'Yes, you are,' he said and stepped aside for them to pass.

Myra ventured a backward look at the spy. He was staring after them, a cold stare that seemed to be trying to see right into her mind – as if he wanted to find out whether her answers were as innocent as they seemed or if she had a hidden motive for her interest in the keys.

Myra stumbled after Dorothy feeling very silly.

Joyce said, 'Was he . . . ?'

'Yes,' said Myra. 'Sssh, he'll hear you.'

'But he's in the Air Force. He can't be . . .'

'I know. But what was he doing spying on the Barracks. 'Course, he could be using his uniform as a disguise.'

But she didn't even convince herself, she'd started the gang on a wild goose chase. He couldn't possibly be a spy if he was an ATC officer. Surely he would have had to go through all kinds of tests? What a good thing she hadn't gone to the police, it would be bad enough explaining this to Eddie and Denis.

Dorothy, curious, said, 'How do you know him? What's this about keys?'

Myra explained how she'd met him in the lane, but thought it best not to say anything about her suspicions.

'Oh!' Dorothy lost interest in the subject. 'Here we are. In here.'

They went into one of the classrooms. Two older boys in ATC air-force blue waited at the front. There were a few girls already seated at desks.

Dorothy introduced Myra and Joyce, saying that they were interested in joining them.

'So you want to learn how to send Morse, do you?.' the taller of the cadets said with a smirk. 'Well, we'll have a go. By the way, I'm called Roger and this is Ted. Okay, take a seat at one of the desks.'

Myra felt like hitting his smug face. It was so obvious that he thought girls wouldn't be any good at this sort of thing. But she allowed Dorothy to lead them to a desk at the back of the room. They were like the ones they'd had in Gladstone, with a ledge underneath for books and an inkwell for each of the two pupils it seated.

Ted came round and gave them each a paper with the Morse code printed on it and a very simple piece of equipment – a flat piece of wood with a lever on top.

'You just press that down and it'll buzz,' he said. 'Keep it down for a second to make a dot and hold it a bit longer for a dash. It's quite easy – not as hard as Roger tries to make out.'

There were only ten girls altogether. Perhaps when Dorothy had written her article about the JACs in their form magazine they might recruit a few more, Myra thought.

'Now,' said Roger, 'I want the new girls to learn the symbols for each letter off by heart by next Friday, but for the time being you can practise sending and receiving with your partner, using the paper.'

After about half an hour taking turns using the buzzer, Ted came and collected them up.

'You can keep the papers with the Morse code on, but bring them with you next week. Okay? And I expect you all to know it by then – without looking at the paper.' Roger gave them the kind of look which said he didn't think they'd do it – that he knew he was wasting his time.

Next, he brought out pictures of British and German planes.

'Study these and see if you can find any differences which will help you identify them. This Lysander, for instance, you can see they have what we call spats over the wheels. It's the only plane that has them. I'll give you half an hour to study them, then I'll test you to see how many you can remember.'

Roger and Ted retreated to a corner of the room.

Myra looked closely at the pictures. 'There's not all that much difference, is there?' she whispered to Joyce.

'Well, that one's got a different-shaped tail. What is it? A Halifax. And that Lancaster's tail is a bit different too.'

Myra was relieved when their time was up. She couldn't dredge up much interest in plane spotting and was glad when they went out into the yard and learned to march in line, form fours, about turn and left and right incline.

What a boring evening, she thought. I'd rather be a nurse than a WAAF. Perhaps next week will be better though, if we go to Pengam aerodrome as Roger said we would. I wouldn't mind learning how to handle a machine gun or pack parachutes. And maybe we'll be able to have a go in that Link Trainer plane, like he said.

As they walked home together, Dorothy said, 'Well, did you like it? It was good, wasn't it?'

'I like the sound of what we're doing next week,' Myra answered, dodging the question.

'Me too,' said Joyce. 'I wonder if we'll learn to fire the machine gun, too.'

'Shouldn't think so. It would be a waste of ammunition,' Dorothy replied.

When Dorothy left them, Joyce returned to the subject of the spy.

'He can't be a spy after all. We better call and tell the boys that it's all off.'

Denis wasn't at home when they called, but Eddie said, 'It still sounds mighty fishy to me. I think we'll still keep an eye on him. We don't want him to get away.'

They told him about their evening and he was amazed when he heard that they were going to learn about machine guns.

'Lucky dabs!' he said. Then after a moment's thought, 'D'you think if I joined the ATC, they'd do it too?'

'I expect so,' said Joyce. 'Ask Denis if he'd like to go with you.'

Myra was glad that they'd had something of interest to tell the boys. She was still feeling rather silly about mistaking the ATC officer for a spy.

The following Friday morning Peter, dressed in his best clothes and with a brown luggage-label tied around his neck, was ready to leave for an unknown destination in the country. He looked very small and frightened. He walked down the street with Mam, insisting on carrying the case that held his clothes, even though Mam had offered to carry it for him. He hadn't cried, he was determined to be brave like the soldiers his mother had told him about.

They were to meet the other children being evacuated at Gladstone School, then they'd all go together to Queen Street station. Myra knew that lots of them would be boys from his class, so there'd be kids he knew and at least he should be safe where he was going. They'd heard a rumour that they would be taken to Llanharan, a village not far from Cardiff, where no bombs had been dropped, there were no military targets and the only factory was one where they bottled milk. Mam was going to be able to visit him when he'd settled in. But it would be very quiet in the house without him. Myra hoped he'd be okay.

Myra watched and waved until they'd turned the corner, then set off for school. She wished there was something she could do to help end the war quickly, but she was too young to join any of the services or even to be a nurse. Well, she'd just have to go on, keeping her eyes open, like the posters said. She still wasn't sure about that man and his strange behaviour, though.

That evening they all went over to Tremorfa to Pengam aerodrome. Roger was showing off, bossing them about in front of the Air Force man who had come to explain where everything was kept.

Roger lay on the ground showing them the correct position to fire the gun, then made them all do the same in turn, shouting at those who didn't get it quite right.

Then he demonstrated how to take a machine gun apart, placing the pieces on a cloth on the ground in the order they had come off.

'Now you do it,' he barked at Myra after he had put it back together again.

She thought she had a good idea how to do it, but then found that she had missed out a piece.

'Sorry,' she muttered, when he snatched it off her, scornfully.

When all the girls had had a turn they were taken into a hangar where women in WAAF uniform were folding and packing parachutes at very long tables.

One of them said, 'They must be folded and packed exactly right and kept dry, too, or they won't open – and that could cost someone his life.'

There was a queue to go in the Link Trainer plane. Several groups of ATC were at the aerodrome that day, so they had to wait.

'Ever been up in a plane?' Ted asked Myra.

She shook her head.

'I have,' he said. 'Look up there!'

Soundless above them a plane with extra long wings glided steadily downwards.

'It's a glider. I've been up in one,' he said. 'It's great. It must be what it's like to be a bird. No noise, just the air rushing past you.'

Joyce decided to stand in the queue, but Myra, curious about the glider, walked with Ted to where they could see it land, smoothly and silently.

As they watched they saw an ATC boy climb out of the plane and then, a few moments later, an older man in the same uniform disembarked.

There was something familiar about his figure. She'd seen him somewhere before. Then he turned and she saw his face – the steel-rimmed glasses. It was the man she'd thought was a spy.

But then, with a shock, she saw him pull something over his head – the strap of a camera he'd had hung around his neck. He must have been taking photographs of the docks up there – the way that German spy had done just before the war started.

Her suspicions flooded back. She hadn't been wrong about him. It all fitted together too well. He was probably sending information to Germany – perhaps that's how they'd bombed that ship when Eddie's father had been killed.

'Look!' Urgently, she shook Ted's arm. 'That man that's just got out of the plane. He's got a camera. He's been taking photographs from up there. He's a spy!'

Ted snorted derisively. 'Don't be so soft. You don't know what you're on about. He's a lecturer. He's probably been taking the pictures to show us.'

'Anyway, come on,' said Ted. 'It must be about our turn to go in the Link Trainer.' He turned and began to sprint back the way they had come.

'Sorry,' Roger said, as he dismounted the steps from the Link Trainer. 'There won't be time for all of you to have a turn. Is there anyone desperate to have a go? There's only time for one more.'

Myra shook her head. If she didn't go in that thing she might have a minute to see where that officer went. See what he was up to – whatever Ted said, she wasn't convinced.

Joyce put her hand up. 'I'd like to have a go.'

Oh, dash, Myra thought. I wanted her to come with me.

'Come on, then,' Roger said, and helped Joyce into the short plane body.

By the time Myra had sprinted back to where the glider had landed, the man was nowhere in sight.

'Can I help you, miss?' a man with Leading Aircraftsman's stripes on his arm asked.

'I'm looking for a man I saw just now,' she said. 'He took a boy up in a glider.'

'Oh, you mean the Flight Lieutenant! He's just gone, I think. Nice gentleman, he is.'

'Oh, I see. Thanks.'

Disconsolately, Myra wandered back to the Link Trainer just in time to see Joyce come out, laughing at something Roger had said. How could she stand him? As her mother would have said, 'he needed to be taken down a peg or two.'

And Myra could think of someone else she'd like to take down a bit, too.

Chapter 6

When Myra told Joyce about the Flight Lieutenant, she said, 'Oh, I wish I hadn't gone in that Link Trainer. Something always happens when I'm not there.'

'I think we better get the gang together, make some plans. There's something fishy about that man.'

By the time they arrived home it was too late to get in touch with the others, but Myra called to Eddie over the wall next morning.

'We'll need somewhere private to talk,' she told him. 'This is strictly secret. We can't have anyone overhearing.'

'How about my Dad's pigeon loft? There's plenty of space underneath and no one will be around. Mam always goes out with *him* on a Saturday afternoon.' Eddie's face darkened as he spoke about his mother's lodger. When his father was alive, he had spent all his spare time at the loft at the bottom of the garden, feeding and training their homing pigeons. Myra remembered that terrible afternoon when Eddie arrived home from school, only to learn that his mother had asked George Slater, the docker billeted on them, to get rid of his father's pets. She'd meant Slater to sell them, but Eddie had gone to the pigeon loft and found their limp bodies. Slater had wrung their necks.

Eddie had hated the man ever since. His mother said,

'Oh dear, he must have misunderstood! I meant him to sell them for me. I'm so sorry, Eddie.'

Eddie said, 'He knew what he was doing. He did it on purpose. He's a cruel . . .'

Mrs Goodwin had cut him short, 'Now, stop it. Eddie. I know you don't like him, but I'm sure he wouldn't do a thing like that.'

But Eddie believed otherwise.

'Good idea,' Myra said. 'But are you sure? Is there room for us all?'

'Yeah. There's loads of space. *He's* got some stuff stored there, but there's still room.'

They waited until they saw Mrs Goodwin and her lodger walk down the street together, Eddie's mother's tiny figure dressed in her best navy costume, twin fox furs draped over her shoulders, tottering along on high heels beside the burly docker.

The afternoon was drizzly, so it was good to have somewhere dry to go. The smell of corn still filled the small space, mingling with the mouldy odour of rotting wood and soil. Some stuff stacked in a corner covered with a tarpaulin took up a bit of room, but it was big enough for the five of them.

'Looks like he's brought more stuff down here,' Eddie said, frowning. 'Wonder what it is.'

'Never mind him,' Joyce said, 'let's get on with it.'

Myra told the others what she'd seen. 'We've got to do something *now*. If he's been taking photos of the docks or the steel works, he'll let the Jerries know and we'll have terrible raids.'

The others nodded in agreement.

'But what?' Joyce voiced their thoughts.

Eddie and Denis had been keeping a regular watch on Flottmanns, but had rarely seen the man they now knew as the Flight Lieutenant. He'd crossed the yard once or twice and they'd followed him to a house nearby where they thought he must live. But apart from that they knew nothing.

'Pity you didn't ask that chap at the aerodrome more about him,' said Denis. 'He seemed to know him.'

'I didn't have time. I wasn't supposed to be there,' Myra said. But all the same she wished she'd thought of it.

'I wonder . . . if he wears ATC uniform, perhaps he's an officer with them.' He turned to Eddie. 'Maybe we should go along and see?'

'Good idea. Do they meet on Fridays, too?'

'Dunno, but we could find out. Perhaps Dorothy knows.'

They agreed to go on watching the man from behind the cemetery wall and that Joyce and Bernadette would take a turn with them.

'We've got to spend as much time there as we can, so if one of us can't go, someone else will have to stand in. Agreed?'

'He wouldn't recognise me,' protested Myra. 'Anyway, I could disguise myself. Dress up as a boy or something.'

'Nah, you'll ruin everything if he spots you,' Eddie said. 'You leave it to us. You've done your bit.'

'Come on, let's go on watch now,' Eddie said. 'Ma's out, so I've got all the afternoon.'

Myra watched wistfully as her friends walked up the street together. She felt left out.

After the others had gone, Myra went back to her own house. She felt a growing resentment. What right had Denis and Eddie to say she had to stay home? She was the one who'd spotted the spy in the first place and it wasn't likely she would show herself and give the game away.

Shouting to Gillian that she was going out, she hurried after them to the cemetery. She saw the others walking down the main pathway and followed them at a distance.

When they reached the far wall, they seemed to be arguing about something, then Denis and Eddie climbed over the wall and ran across the road. They were going towards the factory! The idiots: they'll give everything away.

She dashed up to Bernadette and Joyce.

'Hey, you weren't supposed to come,' Joyce said.

'Who's going to stop me? And where do those two think they're going?'

'Well, Eddie said . . .' Bernadette began.

'Never mind what Eddie said,' interrupted Myra. 'I was the one who spotted him first, so it's not up to Eddie. Now they're taking over.'

'Yeah, they decided to go in there and say they're looking for their ball. Wouldn't let us go, oh no!' said Joyce.

Myra turned to watch the boys and sighed. They were just turning into the factory gates.

'As long as that's all they do. If they do anything to put him on his guard . . .'

They waited for what seemed ages and it was all Myra could do to stop herself running over there and trying to fetch them back. But *he* might see her!

At last, the boys came out, laughing and pushing each other. Eddie seemed very pleased with himself. 'I thought you were going to stay home?'

'You realise he'll know you now, don't you?' Myra retorted. 'And if he sees us together . . .'

'Wait till you hear what Eddie's done,' Denis said. 'Go on, tell her, Eddie.'

Eddie grinned. 'I talked to him. Well – only asked for my ball back first. But I thought to myself, this isn't going to get us anywhere, so I asked him for a job.' He paused to see Myra's reaction.

'A job?'

'Yeah. I thought to myself, we need to get into this place and have a good look round. I wondered, how could we do that. It was then I had a good idea – if I had a job there I could look in his office, see if there were any papers or stuff. 'Sides, if I had a job, Ma could get rid of old Slater, she wouldn't need his money then.'

'So! You risk putting everything at risk just to get a job! Thanks a lot!'

Myra stormed off, Joyce and Bernadette following, with disdainful looks at the two boys.

Myra cooled down a little as they walked back together. 'I suppose they were only trying to help,' she said. She was remembering how upset Eddie had been after that horrible man had hit him. No wonder he had seized the chance to get rid of him. She should have been more understanding.

'Yeah, but they do try to take over all the time,' said Joyce.

'Where are they now?' Myra asked, not wanting to seem curious and turn around to look for herself.

Joyce glanced over her shoulder. 'They're not there. Gone a different way, I s'pose.'

'Oh, I'll see him later,' Myra said. 'We need to know what that place was like inside.' She didn't want to seem as if she were climbing down.

Saying goodbye to the others, Myra went home to find Gillian in the living room in front of the large mirror, dabbing stuff on her hair from a saucer on the mantelpiece.

'What you doing?' She sniffed. 'What's that?' Then she realised. 'You're bleaching your hair. Mam'll kill you!'

'She won't.' But Gillian didn't sound convincing. 'She won't mind. Zelma in the shop told me how much to use – and her hair looks lovely.'

'It'll all fall out and Martin won't want a baldy girlfriend!'

'Huh! Martin. If he can't be bothered to write to me, I'll find someone else. You know what they say about sailors – a girl in every port, and I'm beginning to think they're right. And, anyway, blondes always seem to have all the fun.'

Myra realised then how hurt Gillian was because she hadn't heard from her boyfriend. She obviously didn't believe her mother's story about not being able to post letters until they reached port.

'It *is* right what Mam says, you know. There's a girl in

our school told us her uncle's in the Navy and his letters all come together because of it.'

'Mmm,' said Gillian absently, concentrating on trying to part the hair on the back of her head evenly. 'Well, we'll see when he comes home, won't we!'

It's no good trying to reason with her, Myra thought. As Mam says she's as stubborn as a mule. When she makes up her mind, nothing will shift her. But she hoped her big sister wasn't going to hurt Martin, he was too nice. She remembered when Gillian had first brought him home, he'd said, 'Why didn't you tell me you had a lovely sister? I wouldn't have known which one of you to choose.'

Of course, Myra had known he was only joking, but she'd liked him ever since.

When Mrs Weaver came home and saw Gillian's hair, she was furious.

'Your lovely hair!' she cried. 'You've ruined it. You'll have to go on doing it now or it'll look awful with black roots – and if you do keep bleaching it, the ends will break and it'll still look awful.'

'It'll be all right,' muttered Gillian. But Myra could tell she hadn't known all this and was regretting bleaching it already.

'Oh, well, on your own head be it!' said her mother – then looked puzzled when Myra laughed.

Myra called Eddie over the wall later when she knew he was back home.

'Sorry for saying that about you getting a job. I'd want to get rid of him, too, if I was you.'

'That's okay. I suppose I was a bit daft, showing myself to the enemy, but it's done now.'

'Which way did you come home? We looked for you.'

Eddie shifted uneasily. 'I suppose I'd better tell you. We waited till the Flight Lieutenant came out and we followed him home. It was great. We dodged behind pillar boxes and stuff when he looked around. Some woman opened the door to him. I expect she's his wife. He said something to her and he looked back again. He didn't see us, though; we was careful and ducked behind a lorry.'

Myra sighed. She wished she could have gone instead of them. She would have put her daps on so she wouldn't make a sound – and she'd have stayed at a distance. It sounded as if they'd been walking too close behind him. She hoped they hadn't made him suspicious.

That evening when Dad came home from work, Mam said, 'There's a letter for you behind the clock.' She gave him a worried look.

He drew the letter out and looked at it, raising his eyebrows when he saw the official OHMS on the front. He slit it open and read.

'Is it?' asked Mam.

'Yes. Got to report the end of next week. Sevenoaks. Wherever that is.'

Myra looked from one to the other. 'What is it? Why have you got to go there?'

'I've been called up, love. I'm going in the army!'

Myra gasped. 'But you're too old!'

Dad grinned. 'They don't seem to think so.'

Mam turned and went into the back kitchen, saying, 'I'll get the tea.'

Dad followed her and Myra could hear him saying, 'Don't worry. I'll be all right. They'll probably put me in the cook house when they hear I'm a dab hand at apple tarts!'

But Myra, putting her head round the door, saw that Mam had her face buried in Dad's shoulder and was crying.

'I was hoping this blessed war would be over before you'd be called up,' she said. 'Now they've got you and my two brothers. Oh, when's it going to end?'

Gillian came downstairs just then and received the full brunt of Mam's tongue when she saw her daughter's blonde curls.

'Don't take on, love,' said Dad. 'You're upset now. You'll get used to it.' And Myra knew he wasn't just referring to Gill's hair. Mam ate hardly anything for tea and she kept surreptitiously dabbing at her eyes. Mam never cried. Was she afraid Dad would get killed? Myra shivered and a hard lump came to her throat: she had difficulty in swallowing her food. Dad tried to make Mam laugh by telling her about the antics his horse had got up to that day, pushing his way into people's doorways and refusing to budge until he was given something to eat, but she could only raise a watery smile.

When they'd finished eating, she said, 'I've got a bit of a headache. I think I'll take an aspirin and lie down for a little while.'

'All right, love,' Dad said. 'You go on up and I'll bring you a cup of tea.'

Myra decided to wash the dishes while Mam and Dad were upstairs and managed to persuade Gillian to dry them. 'Come on,' she said. 'Mam's really upset. It's not fair to leave them till Dad comes down. He's the one we should be worrying about.'

Mam was back on her feet an hour later and although her eyes were still puffy and red, Myra could see she'd put a dab of powder on her nose to take away the shine.

Putting her hand in her pocket, Mam said, 'Oh, I forgot, there was a letter from Peter today. He seems to be settling down. Wants to come home, of course, but he's with some nice people, he says. And they've got a dog, so that's made him happier.'

Peter had been nagging Mam and Dad about having a dog for ages now, Myra remembered, so he was probably over the moon at having one to play with and take for walks.

The days until Dad went away flew by. Mam told the butcher that she wanted to make a special meal for him and Mr Walters let her have a rabbit from 'under the counter'. The grocer produced a large onion which, as Mam said, 'were like gold', so with plenty of vegetables she was able to make a large saucepan of stew.

Even Myra, who hadn't eaten rabbit since Peter had kept a lovely white one in a hutch at the bottom of the garden, felt her mouth water at the smell.

They all went to the station with Dad, even Gillian, who had given up her lunch hour to see him off.

Myra saw the crowds of troops with their kitbags on the platform waiting to board trains. Dad will be like them soon, she thought. He'd be dressed in a rough khaki uniform and he wouldn't look like her father any more. She just hoped they wouldn't send him to fight at the front. She wondered if he was nervous. She couldn't imagine her Dad fighting anyway, he was too gentle. The soldiers carried rifles and she wondered how they could be so light-hearted as they laughed and joked with each other, considering they were probably going to the front line. Then a sergeant came along and shouted at them to board the train and they all scrambled aboard, serious now. How awful, thought Myra, it's bad enough that they're going into battle without being treated like that. Some of them looked very young, not old enough to be in the army. That sickening feeling came over her again, like when she first realised that her Dad might be killed. She prayed that he would come home again safely and soon.

Not usually demonstrative, she surprised her father by giving him a huge hug and kissing him before he climbed aboard the train. She was glad she had when she saw his beaming smile as he waved from a window before turning to go to try and find a seat.

After they had watched the train disappear round the curved track, they walked slowly down the steps and out into the station entrance.

They were just in time to see a convoy of army lorries draw up outside.

They stood for a moment watching as soldiers from the Welsh Regiment jumped down from the lorries and picked up their kitbags. They were blocking the entrance, so Mrs Weaver said, 'We'll wait for a moment until they've gone in.'

Quite a crowd of passengers gathered and watched as the troops formed a line ready to file up on to the platform. Myra glanced around and clutched Gillian's arm when she saw a figure dressed in a black overcoat and Homburg hat standing at the side of the entrance. As if feeling her eyes on him, he turned and she saw the ugly steel-rimmed glasses.

'What's the matter?' said Gillian, frowning.

'That man! The one dressed all in black. He's a spy!'

Gillian laughed. 'Oh, yes – and I'm Hitler.'

'No, honest. I saw him spying on the Barracks – and now he's watching the troops. I bet he's going to tell the Germans and they'll bomb the train – Dad could be killed.'

'Don't be daft – Dad's train has gone.' But she looked thoughtful all the same.

'Oh, you don't believe anything I say – that's why we haven't told anyone. When we catch him they'll have to believe us then.'

'Who's "us"? And how are you going to catch him?'

'Joyce and Bernadette and Eddie and Dennis. We've been following him. At least, not me, 'cos he's seen me and he'd know we're on to him then.'

'You better stop. You'll be getting yourselves into trouble. He could be quite harmless.'

'Yeah? Well listen to this! He works at that factory where that other spy was. I bet there's a load of 'em there – under cover.'

'Well – you better tell Mam. See what she thinks. She could go to the police for you and they'd believe her.'

'Bet she wouldn't believe me, either. You don't!'

'I didn't say that. But you can't arrest a man for looking through the Barracks railings, now can you?'

'You won't say anything to Mam, will you? We want to get him ourselves. You never know, Denis said there might be a reward.'

'Oh, is that all you're doing it for? The money?'

''Course not. But we got to get a bit more evidence first. Wait till the gang know I've seen him watching the soldiers here. They'll be mad they didn't see him. They've only followed him from work to his house so far.'

'You are going to get yourselves into serious trouble if you don't watch out. I still think I ought to tell Mam.'

Gillian looked at her mother standing a little distance away from them. 'But she looks upset – and I don't want to worry her any more. Promise me you won't go following him around – even if the others do.'

'They won't let me,' Myra said.

'Good,' said Gillian. 'Keep it like that.'

Chapter 7

On Friday evening Myra and Joyce set out for the WJAC meeting. Joyce's eyes widened with excitement when Myra told her about seeing the Flight Lieutenant at the station.

'So he *is* watching the Welsh Regiment!' she said.

'I was right first time,' said Myra, bitterly. 'It was him wearing ATC uniform that put me off.'

'I wonder if he'll be there tonight,' Joyce said.

'We'll soon see,' said Myra, as they entered the lobby. But she hesitated when she saw the Flight Lieutenant standing there with their usual officer, just the way they'd been when she'd first joined. It was almost as if he'd been waiting for them.

Looking at him warily, they started to edge past.

'Excuse me, young ladies,' the Flight Lieutenant said. 'I'd like a word with you if you don't mind.'

Oh, crumbs, thought Myra. What did he want? Should they make a run for it.

'I want to know why you and your friends have been following me about,' he said.

'*I* haven't,' said Myra.

'No. You're the young lady I saw in the lane by the barracks when I . . . er . . . dropped my keys, aren't you?'

'Yes,' Myra, said defiantly.

'But this other young lady has been popping up wherever I go – as well as two young fellow-me-lads.'

Joyce burst out, 'We know you're a spy. You've been watching the Welsh Regiment in the Barracks and taking photos from that glider. We know – Myra saw you!'

'Oh, she did, did she? Well, well, you have been vigilant. But I'm sure my friend here can reassure you about that. He's known me for a long time – we were in the Force together.'

The grey-haired officer smiled. 'Yes, I think I can safely say that Mr Grant is not a spy. In fact, he wouldn't want me to tell you this – but he was decorated for bravery for his work in Intelligence. Now what d'you think of that? Still think he's a danger to the community?'

'How do we know you're not a spy, too? You could be making it up,' Joyce challenged him.

'You may have noticed that he limps badly,' the officer continued. 'Well, he got that injury when his plane crashed coming back from France. He lost part of his leg and the sight in his right eye, too – that's when he got his medal.'

'Gosh!' Myra said. 'Really?' She could tell somehow that this man was telling the truth.

'Yes,' said Mr Grant. 'You've been very observant, and I must commend you on your public spiritedness, but I hope we've convinced you that I'm not a spy. I must confess that I have been keeping an eye on the Barracks. Old habits die hard, but my interest was purely academic, if you know what I mean.'

Myra nodded. She didn't really know what 'purely academic' meant, but she thought she understood.

Mr Grant laughed. 'Being followed around by two young ladies is very flattering, but I think people will begin to talk if you carry on doing so much longer.'

Myra looked at Joyce. She was looking as embarrassed as she felt herself.

'W-we weren't sure,' she said. 'I thought at first you must be one, then I saw you in ATC uniform and I thought you couldn't be. Then I saw you come out of the glider with that camera – and I thought I was right first time,' she stopped.

'I was taking photographs, I must admit,' said Mr Grant, 'but I can assure you they were only for showing the cadets what Cardiff looks like from the air. Some of them will soon be old enough to join the RAF and it will give them an idea how to use aerial photography – but I can see how it seemed to you.' He gave Myra a searching look. 'You're very observant, aren't you? Perhaps we have a future Intelligence Officer in you. We'll have to keep an eye on you.'

Myra flushed with pleasure. Perhaps she hadn't been all that silly after all. She could imagine herself being awarded a medal by the King for being extremely brave in finding out some well-kept secret of the Germans and bringing the war to an end quickly. Then her father coming home . . .

She woke from her daydream when she heard Mr Grant saying, '. . . so I can safely say that my period of being observed is over, can I?'

'Y-yes,' she said. 'Sorry – we were wrong.'

'I'm glad you were wrong,' Mr Grant laughed. 'I wouldn't want to be shot as a spy.' Which made Myra blush again and stammer out another apology.

'We'll forget about it. No harm done. Cut along and enjoy your evening now.'

Myra and Joyce scuttled off down the corridor, glad to join in a normal session of sending Morse and plane spotting.

'Wait till we tell the others,' said Joyce.

'Yeah, they'll think I'm an awful idiot.'

'They won't. They thought it would be a good idea to follow him, too.'

Eddie's face fell when they gave him the news, but Denis said, 'You shouldn't have done anything until you had more evidence.'

'That's what we were trying to do, wasn't it?' Joyce countered. 'Find out more about him!'

'Yes, I suppose so. But if I see him on my way home from school I'm going to keep out of his way. I don't want a telling off, too.'

'Oh, he didn't tell us off. He was quite nice about it, wasn't he?' Myra turned to Joyce for confirmation.

'Yeah, he even told Myra that she was very observant – that she should be in Intelligence.'

'Well, not exactly,' began Myra.

'And he said he'd keep an eye on her,' Joyce went on. 'I expect he'll wait till she's old enough and then get her a job.'

Eddie looked impressed, but Denis said, 'Huh, you're making it up.'

Joyce and Denis began to argue, so Myra dragged Joyce away, saying, 'Come on, let's go. If he doesn't want to believe us . . .'

That night the bombers returned. They came quite early without their usual warning of dropping incendiaries first to show up their target. Almost as soon as the siren sounded, huge explosions rent the air. The cups on the dresser in Myra's house rattled and the whole family jumped up.

'Come on, down the shelter, quick!' said Mam.

'Oh, not again,' Myra groaned. 'I can't read my book down there, there's not enough light.'

'Better not to be able to read your book than stay here. Remember what happened to those people who didn't go down the shelter?'

The pom-pom-pom merged with the bass thud of the anti-aircraft guns from further away. The heavy drone of enemy bombers directly overhead made Mam hurry them along. You could always tell the German planes, their brm-brm-brm throb was a much deeper sound than the lighter, continuous hum of the British fighters.

Searchlights criss-crossed the sky as they ran down the garden path and jumped into the dark hole of their shelter.

'Here, light the candle.' Mam held out matches to Gill, then pulled the wooden door over behind her.

Gillian made sure there were no uninvited creatures

with them, before tying her scarf in a turban over her curlers.

'Whew, that was close,' Myra's stomach flipped over as the ground shook with yet another explosion. Was this what it had been like when the bomb dropped on Abbie's house? Myra had never been that nervous in the air raids before – not until Abbie's mother had been killed. She couldn't imagine anything bad happening to herself. How had Abbie felt, she wondered, when she heard that tremendous crash? It seemed impossible that anyone as solid as Mrs Pryce could lie crumpled and broken – just like that baby doll she'd dropped when she was little. She remembered her tears when its china head had shattered. Abbie'd been there when it happened. 'Oh, never mind,' she'd said. 'Perhaps your Mam can glue it together again.' But no one could put Abbie's mother together again.

'That was too close for my liking,' Mam muttered. 'I hope Peter's all right. He should be though, where he is.'

They crouched in the semi-darkness listening to the cacophony outside. Bursts of anti-aircraft fire mingled with the dull crump of bombs exploding round the city. Gillian had her hands over her ears.

Clinging to Mam's hand, Myra stared at the inside of the shelter, trying to find something that would take her mind off what was happening outside. She looked at the large nuts holding the corrugated steel sheets together and remembered the day she turned the corner of her street to see a lorry outside her house unloading them. All the kids had been excited – they wanted to know what they were and what you had to do with them.

Then Dad and Uncle Fred had dug out a rectangle four feet deep, bolted the sheets together and planted them down the hole. They'd put a three inch layer of concrete all the way round inside to ground level to keep them firm. The earth had been piled back on top after that for greater protection. Some people had grown plants like strawberries on top of theirs, but Dad had just sown grass seed.

Myra was roused from her memories by an enormous crash, which seemed to rumble on and on until it finally trembled into silence. Instinctively, they all cwtshed down on the floor and Gillian clasped her arms over her head to shield it. They just lay there, holding each other, until Myra said, 'That sounded like it hit the house!'

She moved towards the door, but Mam said, 'Don't! You might get hurt. All sorts of stuff will be falling.' Her face looked old and strained in the dim glow of the candle.

Myra wondered what they would do if the house were just a heap of rubble like Abigail's had been. Where would they go? She supposed they'd have to spend the night in one of the schools – or go and stay at Nanna's.

Mam said, 'When we get out of here I'll slip round to see if Nanna and Grampy are all right.'

Another bomb whistled down – it sounded very near. Myra tried to reassure herself. At least they were still alive – but for how long, she wondered. What was it people said? You never heard the one that got you. But how did anyone know that? Surely they'd be dead!

At least the Germans hadn't dropped gas. She'd heard tales about the last war and the soldiers in the trenches who were still being treated for mustard gas – those that had escaped with their lives. She remembered the men dressed in hospital blue she'd seen walking along Queen Street, hands on the shoulder of the man in front – because they'd been blinded. Hope Dad's all right, she thought. Remembering those poor wounded soldiers deepened her anxiety about her father. Did they have raids where he was? She'd looked it up on the map and it was quite near London and bombs had rained down on the people there. She'd seen pictures of the damage on the Pathé News.

They hardly ever carried their gas masks now. It had been horrible when she first put hers on. They'd all had to go to Crwys Road School to be fitted and the smell of the rubber had made her feel sick, reminding her of the time she'd had a tooth out in the clinic. She'd been glad to take it off again. She'd felt sorry for the poor little babies, though. While they were there, one had been put inside a large sort of bag with a hand pump at the side to filter the air and a clear panel at the top so the mother could see that her baby was all right. It had cried – afraid of being shut inside it. But at least they hadn't had to use them.

That first Sunday morning when war had been declared, her mother had made her carry her gas mask when she went round to Grampy's to dinner – Eddie and Denis had been in the street and they'd laughed at her. Her face still grew hot at the thought.

At last, near dawn, the sound of the guns and bombs died away and they climbed wearily out of the shelter, almost too afraid to look at their house – but it was still there – they'd escaped the bombers again.

Shouts and whistles rent the semi-darkness. The sky was once more glowing crimson with fire.

'You'd better go and see if you can get a few hours' sleep,' said Mam. 'I'm just going to slip round and see if they're all right in Nanna's. Gill – if you'll go and put the kettle on for some cocoa . . .'

As Myra followed her sister up the garden path, she saw a movement in next door's garden. Part of the wall had fallen down ages ago and Dad had never found enough time to build it up again. Peering through the gloom, she saw that it was George Slater, Mrs Goodwin's lodger. He was carrying something in his arms – something heavy by the way his knees were buckling and his arms straining. The Goodwins had never had a shelter – Eddie's mother said she wasn't going in one of 'them dark, damp places': she sat under the stairs – said it was as safe as anywhere.

George Slater bent low when he came to the pigeon loft and disappeared under it. I wonder what he keeps under there, thought Myra, but her attention was distracted when Gillian called, impatiently, 'Myra, don't stand there gawping. I'm tired, I want to get to bed.'

The two girls were still up, sipping their cocoa when their mother came back. She was relieved to find that her parents were safe, but on the way home she'd met a warden.

'He said some houses in Cathays Terrace have been flattened. He thinks it was a land mine. No wonder there was such a bang!' She shook her head. 'Poor souls. The wardens and police are starting to move the rubble in case there's anyone underneath still alive. But he didn't seem to think they had a chance.'

The warden had said that the German planes had been targeting the railway, but their bombs had gone astray. How did they know how to find their target in the dark? Myra wondered. Perhaps Eddie was right, that spy in Flottmanns must have made sure those photographs that he took before the war got back to Germany. What a good thing Mr Grant wasn't a spy after all.

Chapter 8

Myra jerked awake, arms flailing, heart pounding like a sledgehammer. She had been pursued by an evil black cloud that was trying to smother her and no matter how hard she ran, it billowed at her heels. Relieved, she looked around her small bedroom. She was okay, it had only been a dream. She could go back to sleep.

But, she couldn't. She tossed and turned. What had Abbie felt like after she'd heard that bomb fall and her mother hadn't come back to her little sister and her in the shelter? Over and over she re-lived the night's raid, heard the scream of bombs dropping and the heavy gun fire, until, completely exhausted, she slept, only to wake with a start at six o'clock

Anxious to find out what exactly had happened in the Terrace last night, she left for school early, half curious, half dreading what she might find after that enormous explosion. Doreen, one of her classmates, lived at the far end of Woodville Road: her house backed on to the Terrace. Had the land mine, or whatever it was, affected her? Turning the corner, she found the road cordoned off and wardens and policemen who were working there wouldn't allow anyone near. Firemen with smoke-blackened faces still played their hoses over the smouldering remains. Homes where they had only yesterday lived and worked. On the end house, the staircase wall was still standing, the wooden steps leading nowhere, the brightly flowered wallpaper incongruous amongst the hillocks of broken stones, bricks and burning timber. A Coronation mug stood intact on a window sill. She turned away from the sight, glass crunching under her feet as she went.

She cut back up the Terrace, deciding to call for Margaret, but there were barricades across Allensbank Road. She couldn't pass. A warden told her a stick of bombs had fallen on several houses in the road and the pub on the corner was damaged.

Seeing the havoc caused in the night, Myra began to worry. Was Margaret all right? Allensbank Road was only round the corner from where she lived. But Myra was relieved to see Margaret in the playground standing in the middle of a group of girls from their form.

'It was awful' she was saying. 'A friend of mine who lives across the road from me – they were in the shelter, luckily – but when they came out, guess what? There was a piece of gravestone on her mother's bed. One of the bombs landed in the cemetery and blew it right through the roof of their house!'

She waited for her audience to be suitably impressed, then went on, 'And one of the wardens told my father that he saw dogs running along Allensbank Road with bones from the graves in their mouths!'

'Ugh! That's awful,' one of the girls said.

'Disgusting!' said another. 'You're making it up.'

'I'm not. On my honour!' said Margaret, drawing a finger across her throat.

A girl who had been listening quietly at the back of

the group, said, 'If you think that's awful, you should hear what my Dad told us. He was on his way home from work,' she swallowed nervously, 'he said there were bodies – or bits of 'em – hanging from the telegraph wires down in Grangetown. Blown up there by the blast!'

They were all quiet for a moment, then one girl whispered, 'Honest?'

'Yeah, he saw them himself. He said it was gruesome, he felt sick. He couldn't eat his breakfast this morning.'

The bell sounded for lessons just then and they turned away to file into school – which hadn't been damaged at all. It was good to be able to settle down to learning how to plot the contours of mountains and hills and forget the horrors of war for a while.

That evening, Myra settled down to do her History homework in her bedroom, but when she heard shouts from next door, she went to look out of her window to see what was happening. She was just in time to see George Slater raise his arm and deal Eddie such a blow to his head that he staggered across the back yard and crashed against the wall.

'You stay out of there, d'you hear me? I won't have you poking around in my things. Now get out of here, and don't let me see you near my stuff again. Cheeky little bleeder!'

Mrs Goodwin, hearing his raised voice, came to the back door. 'What's the matter?' she asked.

'He's been poking around under the loft. I won't have him and those kids messing around in there. It's valuable stuff.' Then, seeing the puzzled look on his landlady's face, 'I know he's been in there. The ground's been trampled by I-don't-know-how-many-feet – and there was silver paper all over the floor.'

'Eddie! Have you been touching Mr Slater's things? After he's been so good to us? I'm surprised at you, I thought you'd be more grateful.' Then, she turned to her lodger and said, 'I'm sorry, George. Come on in and I'll make you a nice cup of tea. You must be tired after working all night.'

Myra clenched her fists angrily and watched as Eddie leaned against the back wall, an arm covering his eyes, his shoulders shaking with sobs. Stupid woman! Couldn't she see what a bully the man was? *Her* mother wouldn't let anyone hit them like that. But she could have kicked herself for breaking up that bar of chocolate Grampy had given her and offering it round.

And why was he kicking up such a fuss over a few boxes of stuff? He'd said they were valuable, but surely if they were, the loft was a bit of a damp place to store them.

She turned away from the window as she heard her mother calling her. She'd ask Eddie later what exactly Mr Slater kept under that pigeon loft.

Eddie denied all knowledge of it, when she asked him next day after tea when they met at the dead wall.

'How did you know he said I'd been touching his things, anyway?' he demanded, and Myra knew she'd made a mistake to ask, because if she knew about the row, she'd also seen him crying – and he wouldn't like that.

'Oh, I heard him shouting and bawling – you couldn't help hearing what he was saying, he was making so much noise.'

She didn't ask him about the deepening purple bruise on his cheek bone where his head had hit the wall.

Eddie nodded, obviously satisfied she hadn't seen him in tears.

'He got this idea I'd been snooping around those things he's got stored down there – and I haven't been down there – not since we had our meeting. What right has he got to tell me not to go down there, anyway! He's only a lodger. I'll be glad when this job's finished, perhaps he'll go back to London after that.'

'Oh, he's not here for good, then?' From the way Mrs Goodwin and her lodger were behaving she thought perhaps Eddie was going to have a stepfather.

'I hope not. If he is, I'll say I'm older than I am and join the Navy or the Air Force. I can't stand him. He's a bully and Ma don't think he can do anything wrong – that's the trouble.'

'D'you think he's a crook? The way he was shouting the odds about that stuff down there – it was as if he was scared of you finding something you shouldn't.'

'There's only one way to find out.'

'You mean . . . ?'

'Yeah, want to come and see? We'd have to wait till he goes out. It'd be good wouldn't it, if we could catch him up to something and get him put away?'

'Don't get your hopes up: remember what happened about my "spy".'

Eddie grinned. 'Well, he *was* acting suspicious – and

you never know, I might get a job at Flottmanns out of it.'

'When do we have a look? Shall we tell the rest of the gang?'

'I'll let you know what shift he's on, he always tells Ma so she can get his sandwiches ready. He's on ten till six now, so that's no good, we'll have to wait until he's on two till ten. That'll give us all evening to have a good look.'

'What about Joyce and them, are we going to tell 'em?'

'Yeah, I think so. The more witnesses we got the better.'

When she got in later, Myra found her mother sitting at the table scribbling figures. It didn't look as if there would be enough money for the following week.

'What's the matter, Mam?' Myra asked.

'Oh, the usual. Trying to make the money go round. It was bad enough when your father was working, but now he's on Army pay . . .' she sighed. 'He sends me what he can, but it's not much. And what Gillian earns – well by the time she pays her tram fares and has a bit of pocket money herself . . .' She braced her shoulders. 'I think I'm going to have to get a job. There's plenty going, what with munitions and that. But I don't really fancy filling shells with gunpowder. I think I'll ask Auntie Betty if they've got any vacancies in the parachute factory: machining would suit me down to the ground.'

Mam had been a machinist in a shirt factory before

she met Dad and got married and from her tales of what she and the other girls got up to, it had been fun. All she'd had to do was stitch round collars or cuffs – it was called piecework – and the more she churned out, the more she was paid.

Mam hurried round to her parents' house and came back beaming. 'Auntie Bet said they're looking for people now – they've got a rush on. She said I'm sure to be taken on.'

Myra smiled; it was good to see her mother looking so happy.

'How much will you get, Mam? Not as much as in the munitions factory, is it?'

'No, but at least I won't get blown up or get a skin rash from the nasty stuff. Anyway, I'm used to machining – it's my job.' She thought for a moment. 'Will you be all right? I hadn't thought of that. I don't know if it'll be shift work.' A frown creased her forehead at this new worry. Then she smiled again. 'I suppose you could always go to Nanna's – and our Gill will be home by about quarter past six.'

'I'm not a baby, Mam. I can look after myself. I could get the tea ready if you told me what we're having. I can make scrambled egg or omelette with dried egg – and I've done cookery in school, don't forget!'

Mam smiled. 'Of course you can. I keep forgetting you're growing up.'

It seemed very strange to see Mam getting dressed to go out in the mornings, she had always been there in her apron, preparing breakfast and making sure they were clean and tidy for school. Now she had a pinafore over one of her second-best dresses, her hair waved and a dab of powder on her nose.

'It's going to be strange at first,' she told the two girls, 'and I want you both to be as helpful as you can. You can regard it as part of your war effort – it's for your benefit, after all, as much as mine.'

Gillian said, 'Don't forget I don't get home until after six. She's home about four o'clock.'

'Myra's already offered to have tea ready for us by the time we get home, so I don't think it would harm you to give a hand with the dishes, make your bed and do a bit of ironing, do you? And you have a half day on Wednesday.'

'I s'pose so.' Gillian brightened then. 'Not the night I go to the Church Army though!'

'All right, I'll let you off doing the dishes on a Thursday, seeing you won't be here. But I expect you to pull your weight though.'

The next Wednesday, as Myra walked home through the Barracks Lane, she was surprised to see Gillian standing at the end of the lane talking to someone just around the corner. Had she come to meet her from school? It didn't seem likely. Then, as she drew closer, she saw with a shock that she was talking to an American soldier. The Americans had moved into the Barracks when the Welsh Regiment was sent overseas and people were becoming used to seeing GIs round the streets.

Gillian saw Myra and gave her a distant smile, almost

as if she were a slight acquaintance, then turned her back on her.

Myra, her cheeks burning at her sister's snub, walked past and hurried home. She carried out the tasks her mother had left for her in double-quick time, anger lending speed to her movements.

Just wait till she comes home, she thought. I'll teach her to ignore me.

Gillian came in just before her mother was due home and acted as if nothing had happened.

'Very snooty when we're out, aren't we?' Myra said, hotly. 'You ashamed of me or something?'

'I was talking,' Gillian said, airily.

'Yes, I could see that – and to an American. I'll tell Mam if you don't stop. You know what they'll say about you. You know what they say about girls who go out with the Yanks. They'll say you're all out for what you can get.'

'If you do, I'll tell Mam that you're following that man around. See what she says about that!'

'Well, I'm not now, see. He wasn't a spy after all. He used to be an RAF officer. He explained everything. So there!'

Gillian stared at her for a moment, then speaking in a softer tone, said, 'They're quite nice when you get to know them. It's only one or two that give them a bad name. I expect some of our boys are not angels when they're overseas. Don't tell Mam – he's only someone I met in the canteen.'

'What about Martin? Don't you care about him? It was Martin this and Mart that before! You said you were going to marry him when he came home. What's happened to all that?'

'He's forgotten about me. Why should I stay home and be miserable? I bet he enjoys himself when he's in port.'

Just then they heard the front door close and Gillian said, 'Promise you won't tell Mam! I won't hear the last of it.'

Reluctantly, Myra agreed. She didn't want to upset her mother as soon as she came in, but she wished Gill would get a letter from Martin. Perhaps she'd forget all about this Yank then.

Chapter 9

As soon as Eddie heard that George Slater was on the two-till-ten shift, he let Myra and the others know it was safe to investigate the pigeon loft.

'I hope it's still there,' Eddie said. 'I've seen him taking stuff out of there a few times lately, but I didn't have a chance to look and see what it was. Every time I go out the garden for anything, he's there watching me.'

'You sure he's in work now?' Bernadette asked. 'I don't want to get into any trouble.'

'Yes, it's okay. He's gone to work. I saw Ma making his sandwiches. Spam! He gets all the best things. I only get bread and jam.'

'Well, if we get a move on we might be able to find something that'll get rid of him, so come on,' Myra urged. She couldn't wait to take a look at those bundles under the tarpaulin.

'Ma's on her own tonight: she's gone to the pictures, so we've got plenty of time,' Eddie said.

They all trooped down the garden path to the pigeon loft, Myra cwtshing low in case her mother happened to look out of the window.

'Watch out before you touch anything, Eddie,' Denis said. 'We'll have to remember to put everything back as it was or he'll know we've been down here.'

Eddie crouched down to reach under the loft. As he

slowly dragged the tarpaulin off George Slater's 'valuables', the children's eyes widened in surprise. Stacks of tins were gradually revealed. They certainly hadn't expected this – there were huge tins of food stacked on top of one another. Tins like the ones the shops used to slice up and sell to customers by weight. There were large tins of Spam, corned beef and ham. There were smaller tins of peaches and pineapples, packets of dried fruit and even several bottles of whisky.

'What a swizz, it's just old tins of food,' said Joyce, disappointed. 'I thought it would be guns or ammunition, something like that. Something exciting. What's he going to do with all this food?'

'What d'you think!' exploded Denis. 'Sell it on the black market, of course. I bet he's been pinching it off the ships he's been unloading. Taking food that belongs to all of us, kinds we haven't seen for ages – and making a packet from it.'

'What d'you mean "the black market"?' asked Bernadette.

'For goodness' sake!' hissed Denis. 'It's when people sell food they're not supposed to have. Food that's been pinched usually – food that's rationed. Haven't you heard of that? And usually they get a lot of money for it.'

'Oh, you mean like when the grocer gives my mother a bit extra from under the counter because he knows we're a big family? But he doesn't charge us any more, I don't think.'

'Something like that, but he's just being kind.'

'What shall we do?' asked Myra. She hadn't been expecting to see food either.

'Go to the police,' Denis said. 'This should put him away for a long time.'

'Did I ought to tell Ma first?' wondered Eddie. 'She'll be mad if she comes home and finds a policeman in the house. She'd blame me.'

'They won't believe us, anyway,' said Joyce. 'I mean, food in a pigeon loft. They'd think we were having them on.'

It had all seemed so easy when the idea had first occurred to them, but now doubts were beginning to settle on the little group.

'Look,' said Denis. 'You want to get rid of old Slater, don't you, Eddie? Well, we got to tell someone – someone who'll believe us and do something about it.'

'Yes, but who?' Joyce asked.

'I know who we could tell,' said Myra quietly.

'Who?' said Denis.

'Mr Grant. He used to be in Intelligence, he'd know what to do.'

'Yeah! Good idea,' said Joyce. 'We could ask him tomorrow night. It's too late to do anything tonight anyway.'

'Don't tell anyone else, mind,' said Denis. 'We don't want it getting back to old Slater and warning him off.'

'No, don't tell anyone,' Myra agreed. 'He'd take it out on Eddie if he knew we'd been down here again.'

They spread the tarpaulin carefully back over the tins just the way they'd found it and, peering out to make sure there were no neighbours around, left the garden.

'Do you want me and Joyce to see what Mr Grant says tomorrow night – or do you two want to be in on

90

it?' Myra asked Eddie and Denis. They knew Bernadette wouldn't be able to come, she always had to look after the baby on a Friday night.

'We'll come,' Eddie and Denis said together.

'Right, call for us at quarter to seven, and don't be late,' Myra said, 'Mr Grant is usually in the lobby when we go in at seven.'

'What were you doing down next door's garden?' Gillian asked, when Myra went home.

'You been spying on me?'

'No – I was looking out of my bedroom window and saw you all trooping down there. What were you doing?'

'Nothing – just talking.'

Gillian lifted her eyebrows quizzically. 'Not talking about catching spies again, I hope.'

'I told you he wasn't a spy, after all. We don't follow him any more.'

Their mother came in from work just then and, after hanging up her coat and hat, she took a letter out of her handbag, saying, 'I've had a letter from your Dad.'

'Oh, good,' Myra said. 'What's he say?'

'He's fine – they've been teaching him to drive. Isn't that nice? Perhaps after this old war's over we'll have a little car and be able to go to the seaside on his half day – and maybe he won't have to drive that horse and van any more. He might even get a motorised van.'

Mam took a closer look at Gillian. 'What on earth have you done to your face?'

Gillian had painted her lips a vivid scarlet, plucked her eyebrows to a thin line and her cheeks were pink with rouge. Her blonde hair had been combed to cover one eye in a style worn by her favourite film star, Veronica Lake.

'Go and wash it off straight away,' ordered her mother. 'You look like a painted doll – and put a clip in that hair. You'll go cross-eyed wearing it like that!'

'But Mam,' wailed Gillian. 'It's modern. All the girls wear make-up!'

'Well, you're not,' said her mother. 'Go and wash it off this minute. You've got a lovely complexion and I'm not going to let you ruin it with all that muck.'

Gillian stormed out to the back kitchen to wash it off. Myra could hear her muttering to herself, 'I'll only put it on in work. See if I don't.'

But whether her mother heard her or chose not to, she didn't know. Mam was reading Dad's letter again and smiling, obviously happy to know he was well and that he was learning to drive – and contemplating the new horizons it might open to them. But Myra had darker thoughts. She recalled seeing those soldiers in the back of Army lorries. What if he was posted overseas and had to take them to the front line? He'd be in terrible danger then. That idea had probably not occurred to her mother.

When Gillian came back into the living room, her face scrubbed clean and shining, she went to her handbag and drew out a small packet.

'Look what I had given to me!' she said, waving it defiantly in front of her mother.

'What is it?' Mam said, frowning.

'Silk stockings!' Gillian gave a triumphant smile at the expression on their faces. 'I'll keep them for when I go out somewhere special. And I had this!' She produced some bars of chocolate and offered them to Myra and her mother.

'Where did you get those?' Mam asked.

'Oh, in the Church Army last week. Nice, aren't they? You can have the chocolate, I'm slimming.'

'Who gave them to you? You can't get silk stockings any more.'

'Oh, one of the chaps there had them. They can get them in their canteen.'

'American, was he?'

Yes – and I know what you're going to say. But he's really nice, you'd like him.'

'I'm not so sure. Why is he giving you these things? He doesn't know you – or does he? Have you been out with him?'

'Not exactly. I met him up by the Barracks and we got talking.'

'He picked you up, in other words. What about Martin? You were full of getting married to him only a few weeks ago, you fickle girl.'

'He's probably married,' Myra said. 'He's probably got a wife back in the States – and six kids, too, I shouldn't wonder. You know what they're like, they'll tell you anything.'

Gillian's mouth set in a mutinous line. 'He's not like that, he's nice. He said his Dad's got a ranch, he showed me a picture of himself dressed in cowboy clothes.'

'He was probably working there,' Myra said.

'Have you thought how Martin would feel if he knew you were seeing this young man while he's away at sea fighting for his country? It would break his heart!'

'If he can't be bothered to write to me . . .' Gillian muttered, 'why shouldn't I enjoy myself.'

'Go away and think about it. Imagine how you'd feel if the boot was on the other foot.'

Gillian stuck her nose in the air and left the living room. They heard her climbing the stairs, then the door of her bedroom slammed shut.

'That girl!' said Mam. 'She'll be the death of me.'

Eddie and Denis called for Myra and Joyce on time, then they walked together to Allensbank School. They argued for a while as to whether the boys should wait outside – since the JACS was for girls – or whether they would all go in together.

'Oh, come on,' Eddie said. 'We'll never get anywhere like this.' He strode into the lobby.

Two officers stood there. Eddie stared at them. He didn't recognise either of them – neither had on the distinctive steel-rimmed glasses Mr Grant always wore.

He turned to go back out again and bumped into the other three on their way in.

'He's not there!'

Joyce walked up to the two officers. 'Is Mr Grant here?'

'No, Mr Grant's not coming tonight. I'm taking his place,' said one.

Seeing their crestfallen looks, the officer said, 'Can I help?'

'No, thank you,' Myra said. 'It has to be Mr Grant.'

'Can I give him a message?'

'We wanted to see him specially – it's important.'

'If I see him later I'll tell him.'

There was nothing more to be done so they trooped back outside.

'Now what we going to do?' Eddie said.

'You two go on in and we'll have a think,' Denis said. 'We might hit on a good idea.'

Myra and Joyce went into the classroom, but neither could concentrate properly on what they were doing, earning themselves a reproof from Roger for getting the name of a Hurricane wrong in plane-spotting.

Denis and Eddie were waiting for them when the session finished.

'Well, did you come up with any bright ideas?' Joyce said.

'As a matter of fact,' said Denis, loftily. 'We think we have.'

'Well, spit it out,' Myra said, impatiently.

'Eddie thought he'd have a look round old Slater's bedroom when he's out – you know, see if there's anything there that could give us a clue to what he's up to.'

'And what's that going to do?' Joyce said. 'We know he must be selling the stuff on the black market.'

'You never know – there might be something. Anyway, you got a better idea?' Denis snapped back.

'Not yet,' said Joyce. 'I'll have a think. I should be able to do better than that, though.'

'What if Mr Slater finds out?' Myra said, remembering how he'd reacted when he thought Eddie had been looking at his things under the pigeon loft.

'I'll be careful. I'll make sure everything's back exactly as it was.' Eddie had that stubborn look on his face again and Myra knew that nothing would stop him.

'When will you do it? It's too late tonight, he'll be home soon,' Denis said.

'If he's in work tomorrow – I'll do it then. The sooner the better.'

Myra didn't like the idea much. She'd seen how George Slater treated Eddie when he had only a suspicion. If he caught him going through stuff in his bedroom, he'd be sure to start knocking him about again.

'Make sure he's not anywhere around then,' she said. 'If you like I'll keep a look-out for you in the street, then if I see him coming, I'll nip through the house and call you out the back. Okay?'

Eddie gave her a grateful look, 'Right. I'll let you know. It'll probably be tomorrow night. Ma generally goes to the pictures on a Saturday, so there'll be nobody there.'

The following evening, everything worked out as planned. George Slater was working an extra shift, and Mrs Goodwin went off to the pictures. Myra stood outside her front door, looking up and down the street.

After about half an hour, when she was getting fed up with her vigil, Eddie opened his front door, an excited look on his face.

'You should see what I've found,' he said. 'Come round the back.' He disappeared behind his front door again and Myra ran through her house to meet him in the back garden.

'What d'you find?' she asked, breathlessly.

Eddie had been concealing something behind his back. He brought it out with a flourish which would have done credit to a conjurer, unfolded the cloth that covered it, and revealed a gun.

Chapter 10

'Where d'you find that? It's not loaded is it?' Myra backed away.

'Dunno. It was in the bottom of his wardrobe. I'm not kidding I was dead scared he'd come back while I was looking in there.' Eddie turned the revolver over in his hands. 'I wonder where he pinched this from? It's a Smith and Wesson .38. Look it says here.'

'What you going to do with it now? Put it back?' Myra wasn't interested in the make – all she wanted to do was to get rid of the thing.

'No. I'm going to hide it. It's proof he's a crook. He wouldn't have a gun if he wasn't a crook.'

'Where shall we hide it? I don't think I'd better have it. Mam'd go mad.'

Eddie looked around. His eyes lighted on the pigeon loft. 'In there. He'd never think of looking there.'

'What if he notices it's missing? He'll go for you again.'

'He's not likely to go looking for it tonight, is he? And I'll make sure I'm fast asleep by the time he comes back. And even if he looked in my room he wouldn't find it there, would he?' Eddie grinned.

They hid the revolver in a corner under a heap of straw, so close to George Slater's cache that he'd never think of looking for it there.

'We going to tell the others?' Myra asked. She was very nervous about hiding this gun. There'd be terrible trouble if the man found it was missing. There would be safety in numbers if the others were in on it too. But Eddie said, 'Let's keep it between us for now. After all, you helped me and I'm the one taking all the risks.'

Myra knew that Eddie was a bit jealous of Denis and wanted to keep his find to himself. Denis always tried to take over when anything was going on, and Eddie resented it.

'Okay,' she agreed at last. 'What's the time? When d'you think he'll be back?'

'Dunno. He was working an extra shift, so it might be a short one. We better get out of here, in case he comes in.'

Saying goodnight to Eddie, Myra scrambled back home over the broken-down wall and went in to the kitchen. Gillian was standing in front of the mirror as usual, combing her hair and gazing at her reflection from all angles. Suddenly, she gave a cry.

'When did this come?' She slid an envelope from behind the clock on the mantelpiece.

'Dunno,' said Myra. 'What is it?' She had too many other things on her mind to bother with Gillian.

'It's from Martin. Look!' Myra saw that her fingers were shaking as she tore open the envelope and began to read. She sank into an easy chair, her face first pale, then flushed.

'His ship was torpedoed,' she said, tears beginning to well in her eyes. 'He's been in hospital. Oh, and I thought he couldn't be bothered to write.' She turned to the letter again, reading it through avidly.

'He's coming home! What date is this?' Gillian glanced at the envelope.' It's this weekend! Goodness – I'd better wash my hair. And what can I wear? I wish I had something new – I'll have to give my best dress a press, that's all . . .'

Myra laughed. Good! Martin was safe and Gill had forgotten the GI already.

'Where's Mam?' she asked Gillian.

'Gone to see Nanna. She said not to be late going to bed. I wonder why she didn't tell me there was a letter for me? Perhaps she just forgot.' But Gillian's mind was already on other things, so Myra turned on the wireless to listen to Saturday Night Theatre.

She knew she wouldn't sleep until she heard that George Slater was home and Eddie safe in bed. If he found that gun was missing they'd hear him all over the neighbourhood.

Myra heard her mother come home and listened to the sound of voices from downstairs. She heard Gillian's raised voice and her mother's quieter tones. Then Gill's voice became quieter, too and one after the other she heard them coming upstairs. She raised herself from the pillow as Mam popped her head round the door.

'You asleep?' Mam whispered.

'Not yet. Did Gill tell you about Martin?'

'Yes,' Her mother gave a wry smile. 'I'm in the dog-house for not telling her there was a letter for her. But I went out in a hurry . . .'

'He was torpedoed. I'm glad he's okay, though. I 'spect she'll give that Yank the push now, do you?'

'I hope so. Go to sleep now. Night-night.'

'Night-night, Mam,' Myra murmured, determined to stay awake in case there were sounds from next door. But in the end, her eyelids drooped – and she was fast asleep.

As soon as Myra woke she went to her window and peeped out at Eddie's house. George Slater's curtains were drawn. Eddie's bedroom window was directly opposite hers and his curtains, too, were closed. Myra heaved a sigh. She wondered if George Slater often checked on that gun, or if he was so confident that no one would dare go through his things that he didn't bother. She crossed her fingers.

Gillian was still grumbling at Mam because she'd forgotten to tell her about Martin's letter, but soon was too busy making herself glamorous for her boyfriend, washing her hair, doing her nails and pressing her clothes that she soon forgot about it in her excitement.

'Which d'you think?' she asked them, holding up two dresses in front of her. 'This one or this one? Oh, I wish I had some coupons!'

'You look very nice in either,' said Mam. 'Anyway, Martin won't notice your clothes. It's you he wants to see. What time's he coming?'

'About eleven. What time's it now? I'll have to hurry.'

They were startled by a roar from next door.

'Oh, that man's off again,' said Mam. 'How Mrs Goodwin puts up with him, I'll never know. He's always shouting and bawling about something.'

Myra's heart fluttered. Had he found his gun was missing? She restrained the impulse to rush outside to see if she could hear what was going on, but when it quietened a little, she went out into the garden and stood in the shadow of the high wall that divided the two houses.

Their kitchen window was open. Myra could hear Mrs Goodwin bleating something, then George Slater's rough voice thundering, 'The little b . . . ! He's been in my room I tell you. Wait till I lay my hands on him. I'll give him snoop, he won't know what's hit him.'

'I'll talk to him,' Mrs Goodwin said. 'He's missing his father. You sure he's been in your room? He hasn't taken anything, has he?'

'I can see someone's been rummaging in there. The things in my wardrobe are all over the place.'

Oh, yes, thought Myra. You wouldn't want to tell her you had a gun in there, would you? And now it's missing. Her stomach turned over as she thought about what the man might do to her friend.

She could see that Eddie's curtains were still drawn. Was he still in bed? If so, it was a wonder old Slater hadn't gone in there and dragged him out – and surely he'd heard the noise!

'He's not in his room I tell you,' Mrs Goodwin protested. 'I've just been up to look and his bed hasn't been slept in. Oh, don't say he's run away.' Her voice rose hysterically. 'Oh, why did you beat him, George?

He's a good boy. His father never laid a finger on him – and you'd no business to. He's nothing to do with you. If anything happens to him, I'll never forgive you. He's been so unhappy.'

'I'll make him unhappy when I get hold of him. Where's he likely to be? Who're his friends?'

'Only the children in the street and I know their mothers wouldn't encourage him to stay.'

'Tell me their names – I'll soon find out.'

Myra was scared when she heard Mrs Goodwin say, 'Well, there's the little girl next door and two others who live up the street – oh, and another boy, Denis. He lives just round the corner. But I tell you their mothers wouldn't allow him to stay with them. Oh, I'm so afraid he's run away. What can I do!' And Myra heard Eddie's mother begin to sob. 'He's been wanting to join the Navy, but surely they wouldn't take him? He's too young.'

'They'll hammer some discipline into him if they have. Oh, stop snivelling, woman; I can't stand that caterwauling!'

'I told you you'd been too hard on him, George. He's only a young lad. They all get up to mischief at times.'

'Ah, you're too soft with him. My father used to knock me about something terrible, but it didn't do me any harm. Toughened me up – and that's what your lad wants.'

Myra wondered where Eddie had gone. His mother had said he wasn't in his bedroom. Had he really run away? Where would he go?

She heard a banging at her front door.

'Myra!' Her mother called. 'I'm upstairs with Gillian. Answer the door, will you?'

Myra didn't reply at once. She was afraid it was George Slater.

'Myra! D'you hear me?'

'Okay, Mam. I'm going.'

With dragging feet, she walked through the long passage. It might be someone else, she reassured herself. But when she opened the door, she trembled when she saw Mr Slater towering over her. He leaned his ham-like fists on each side of the doorway as if barring her way. His large belly was level with her eyes, and she could smell his sweat.

'You seen that Eddie?' he barked.

'No – not today,' she stammered.

'Last night?'

'I haven't seen him since teatime yesterday,' she said.

'You sure?' He stuck his chin out aggressively.

'I'm sure,' Myra whispered. Well, it had been just after tea, she thought, it wasn't really a lie.

'I hope you're telling me the truth,' he said, turning away.

Myra wanted to run up the street and tell the others not to say anything. Then she remembered they didn't know anything about the gun, so he wouldn't be able to force anything out of them. Just as long as Joyce didn't blurt anything out about the stuff he kept under the pigeon loft.

The pigeon loft! Could Eddie be hiding under there?

Myra made sure that Mr Slater was on his way up the street towards Joyce's house, then she ran through her house and down the garden, taking no notice when she heard her mother asking who was at the door.

She called over the wall, 'Eddie, you in there?'

'Ssh,' came his voice. 'I don't want him to know I'm in here.'

'What you gonna do? You'll have to come out some time. Shall I bring you some food?'

'Not now, wait till he's gone out.'

'He's out now. Gone up to see Joyce and Bernadette – to ask 'em if they know where you are. He's been to my house.'

'What you say?'

'Told him I hadn't seen you since teatime yesterday. Your mother thinks you've run away.'

'Good. I'm trying to think what to do.'

Myra could just see the pale blur of Eddie's face in the dark corner.

'Turn away and sit on the wall, then, if they're looking out the window, they won't guess I'm here,' he said.

Obediently, Myra turned away and was just about to ask Eddie if he wanted her to go to the police, when she heard George Slater's loud voice through the open door of Mrs Goodwin's back kitchen.

'I bet I know where the little heller is. Hiding under the pigeon loft! He's been down there before. Let me get my hands on him.'

Myra ducked down behind the wall, just in time. Slater was coming down the path! Should she go and call the police? But the police station was at least five minutes away, even if she ran – he could beat Eddie to a pulp by then.

She peeped over the wall just in time to see the burly docker stoop and enter the dark space below the loft next door and in no time he had Eddie by his collar and was dragging him out.

'Think you can hide from me, do you?' he said, giving Eddie a clout across his ear. 'I'll teach you to go through my things. Private property, that is. What you done with it, eh?' he said, whacking Eddie across his bottom.

'Don't know what you're talking about,' Eddie said, defiantly.

'Oh, you don't, do you? Funny thing it was there when I went out last night – and now it's gone. Who took it? Your mother, eh?' Slater shook Eddie violently, making his teeth chatter.

When Eddie refused to answer him, he raised his fist and punched him. Myra saw Eddie's knees buckle and knew she'd have to do something. His mother was skulking in the house, pretending she didn't know what was going on, just as she had done for so long.

Myra scrambled to her feet, ran to the broken-down part of the wall, jumped over, then ran under the loft. She searched in the straw for the gun and going outside again, pointed it at the stunned George Slater, shouting, 'Leave him alone, you big bully. Let him go!'

His eyes narrowed. 'Oh, you're the one who's been messing around in my room, are you? Give me that gun before there's an accident.'

It must be loaded, thought Myra, almost dropping it in fright.

'Leave Eddie alone. I'm warning you. I know how to use it. We've been taught in the JACs.'

'Oh yeah? I bet. They wouldn't let kids like you handle guns. Give it to me and we won't say any more about it.'

'Oh, you'd like that, wouldn't you! You think I'm going to let you go on beating Eddie like that? We're going to the police. When they hear what you've been doing on the black market and everything, you'll go to jail.'

George Slater's face reddened. 'You little vixen! Give me that gun.' He lunged at Myra, but she stepped back and as she did, tripped over the edging of the path. As she fell, her finger tightened on the trigger and the gun went off.

This stopped Slater for a moment, but then he leapt at her, wrenched the revolver off Myra and dragged her to her feet with his other hand. Eddie, seizing his opportunity, jumped forward, pummeling Slater's back, head and any other part he could reach, so that the man had to let Myra go in order to defend himself.

'Run, Myra!' shouted Eddie. 'Get help!'

But Myra wasn't going to leave him on his own. While Eddie head-butted Slater from behind, she kicked his shins and scratched him like a wild cat. She didn't hear the shouting from her own garden until she was pulled away from Slater. Turning furiously, ready to take on yet another opponent, she gasped in amazement and relief to see Mr Grant standing there – and Martin scrambling over the garden wall on his way to join him.

Chapter 11

George Slater shook off the children and tried to run back into the house, but Martin brought him down in a rugby tackle and he and Mr Grant soon had the struggling man safe between them.

Mrs Weaver and Gillian, who had followed the two men out of the house when they heard the shot, looked in amazement at the scene before them. George Slater was still trying to get away, but the two men held him firmly. Eddie picked up the gun that had fallen in the struggle.

'Leave it where it is, son,' said Mr Grant, then turning to Mrs Weaver and Gill, said, 'Would one of you mind calling the police? We'll hold on to him until they come. Tell them to hurry.'

'I'll ask Mrs Hitchen if she'll let me use her telephone,' Gillian said, as she hurried away to the corner shop.

'Got any rope we could use?' Martin asked.

Mrs Goodwin, who had remained safely inside until then, said in apparent astonishment, 'Oh, there you are, Eddie! Thank God you haven't run away! But what's going on? What are they doing to you, George? What's the matter?'

Myra couldn't believe her ears. Now could she not have heard that gun shot? Martin and Mr Grant had heard it in her house and had come running. She was just covering herself – pretending she didn't know anything about Slater's activities. But Myra knew better. If it wasn't for the fact that she knew it would hurt Eddie, she'd tell the police. Have her put away too.

'He only had a gun, Ma! That's what's the matter.'

'A gun? But whatever was he doing with a gun? I don't understand.'

'No, neither do I,' said Mrs Weaver. 'Martin said that was a gun shot. Frightened me to death, it did.' She put her hand to her chest, 'Oh, it's brought on my palpitations.'

'Go and put the kettle on, Myra, and make a cup of tea for your mother,' Mr Grant said. 'You can tell us what this is all about after we've got this chap inside – and Eddie, find us that rope, will you?'

It took all Mr Grant's and Martin's strength to hold the burly docker as he cursed and swore, twisted and turned to get away. Eddie rummaged in a corner of the loft and eventually brought out a length of clothes line. Mr Grant tied Slater's wrists while Martin held him.

Myra climbed over the wall to her own garden and went into the house. As she filled the kettle she noticed her hands were trembling. 'No wonder,' she muttered to herself. She'd been nervous about Eddie hiding that gun from the start, but if she'd known how it would all turn out, she'd never have agreed.

And how had Mr Grant turned up in the house? He'd been in Intelligence, of course, but how had he learned about George Slater's shady dealings?

Gillian came panting back in, 'They're coming, I think I heard the police car's bell as I came in.'

'You'd better go and let them in then,' Myra said.

Gillian looked in the mirror and patted her hair into place before going back to the front door. The knocker sounded just as she reached it.

Myra heard the deep rumble of a man's voice, then the heavy tread of boots coming through the passageway.

'Where is he?'

'Through here,' Gillian said, leading the way.

'Well,' muttered Myra, 'never mind about me. I'm only the one who might have got shot. I'm only the one who's done all the dirty work. You carry on Myra, you make the tea, while everyone else takes over.'

She heard the sound of the policemen's voices as they took George Slater into the house next door, Mrs Goodwin's fluttering voice protesting. Her mother and Gillian came back in.

'Well, did you ever! Where's that cup of tea, Myra. I need something to steady my nerves.' Mam sank into her chair, fanning her face with her hand. 'Now, are you going to tell me just how you got caught up in all this? What's been going on? I never did like that man – a proper bully, he is!'

'How come Mr Grant was here?' Myra asked. 'Has he gone to the station with the policemen?'

'I don't know,' Mam said. 'They're all in Mrs Goodwin's at the moment.'

Martin's head poked round the back door. He put his arm around Myra's shoulders and said, 'You all right, kid?'

Myra grinned at him, suddenly feeling better. 'Yeah, okay. It was a bit scary though, when I tripped and that gun went off. I was scared in case I'd shot somebody.'

'You had the gun? Oh, my goodness!' Mam flopped back in her chair and fanned herself again. 'What were you doing with a gun? Where did you get it?'

'Eddie found it in the wardrobe in old Slater's room – and we hid it.'

'Why did you do that? You should have told his mother.'

'His mother!' Myra snorted. 'Fat lot of good that would have been. She can't even stop him knocking Eddie around. I can't see her taking a gun off him.'

'Well, you could have told me!'

'Would you have believed me if I'd told you he's been stealing stuff and selling it on the black market?'

'Is that what he's been doing?' Martin asked.

'We think so. There's a load of stuff down under the pigeon loft. Tins of meat and fruit. Bottles of whiskey.'

'Whew!' Martin gasped. 'No wonder he tried to get away. He'll be put away for a long time. That's nearly as bad as treason in wartime.'

A tap came at the kitchen door and Mr Grant came in. 'Excuse me, but the police have just taken Slater away. I thought I might as well come back the way I went out.'

'Come in, come in.' Mrs Weaver waved a hand towards a chair. 'Sit down, please, Mr er . . .'

'Grant,' supplied Myra. 'He's an officer in the ATC, but he used to be . . .'

Mr Grant cut her short. 'An ATC officer will do nicely, Myra. I expect you're wondering how I came to be here this morning.'

111

Myra nodded.

'My friend, Mr Bennett told me – said you'd been asking after me – and that you seemed to be very worried about something. Knowing your talent for sniffing out spies – I thought I'd better see what you wanted.'

'Spies!' Mam said. 'What's this about spies?'

'Um – a question of mistaken identity,' said Mr Grant. 'But your daughter is a very observant girl, and I knew she wouldn't be anxious over something trivial. So just to be on the safe side, I asked for your address from the WJAC and here I am.'

'Thank goodness you and Martin came in just then. He'd have got the gun off me when I fell and . . .' she couldn't go on. It was too frightening to think about.

'Well, anyway. The police will want to talk to you, probably this afternoon – once they get Slater locked up safely. Would you like me to come with you?' He turned to Mrs Weaver. 'That's if you don't mind.'

'I think a man's presence would be better in the circumstances – and being her Dad's in the Army . . . Of course Martin would go, I'm sure, but he and Gillian haven't seen each other for such a long time. Er – perhaps I'd better come along with you, if I may, just to see what's going on.'

Mr Grant smiled. 'Of course.'

Mrs Goodwin and Eddie went with them to the main police station that afternoon. The policemen who interviewed them were impressed when Mr Grant showed them his identity card.

'Pleased to meet you, sir,' he said.

The policemen asked Myra and Eddie a lot of questions.

'When did you find George Slater's cache of food?'

'Do you know how long it's been there?

'Did you see him put it there?'

'How did you come to find the gun?'

Myra could see her mother's face becoming more and more astonished as she answered the men's questions.

'You could knock me down with a feather,' Mam said. 'I had no idea what they were up to.' And turning to Myra, 'You should have come to me and let me deal with it.'

'I thought you had enough worries,' Myra said. 'You'd probably have told Mrs Goodwin first and she'd have told him and he'd have got rid of it.' Seeing her mother's face, Myra continued, 'Anyway, I was going to tell Mr Grant – he'd have known what to do – but he wasn't there.'

Eddie and Mrs Goodwin were being interviewed in another room and the two families met on the way out. Mrs Goodwin was in tears and Eddie was trying to comfort her.

'I didn't know what George was up to,' she sniffed. 'He was very generous with the tinned stuff. I thought he was kind.'

Eddie and Myra exchanged a look. How could she say that?

Mrs Weaver went to her and put an arm around her shoulders. 'I'm sorry you've had such an experience,' she said. 'Come back to our house and I'll make you a nice cup of tea.'

That was Mam's cure for everything, thought Myra.

Mr Grant escorted them back to their house, but when Mrs Weaver invited him to stay to tea, he excused himself, saying, 'If you don't mind, I must get home. Things to do.'

Martin and Gillian were sitting side by side on the couch when they went in to the living room. Martin was holding Gill's hand and Myra noticed immediately the ring on the third finger of her left hand.

She grinned. 'Wait till Mam sees that,' she murmured. 'What d'you think of her hair, Martin?'

'Very glamorous,' said Martin. 'But she says she's going to grow it out by my next leave.'

Mam came in just in time to hear this. 'That's the most sensible thing she's said for a long time. Spoiling her lovely hair like that!'

Gillian held her hand out towards her mother.

'What's this? Oh, my. Let me see?' She peered at the tiny cluster of diamonds shaped like a flower. 'Very pretty.'

'I hope you don't mind. I should have asked you first, but I was so happy to see Gill again – and I've had it for a while now. I couldn't resist giving it to her.'

'What can I say? I know Gill's been missing you – and you've been through such an awful time – I hope you'll both be very happy.' Seeing their relieved smiles, she added, 'But I hope you don't intend getting married for a year or two. Gill has to prove she's sensible enough first.'

114

'And we have to save for our home, too,' said Martin. 'A sailor's pay is not enough to keep a wife on.'

'Very wise,' said Mam. 'And I've got two bits of news for you, too. First, Peter's passed the secondary school exam and they're sending him home,' she paused for a moment, 'and I've had a letter from your Dad to say he's coming home on leave. It's embarkation leave, I'm afraid, so we'll have to make the most of it.'

'Yippee!' Myra said. They'd be a whole family again, even though Dad would only be home for a short while. It seemed like a promise that one day everything would be back to normal. No more shivering nights in air raid shelters, no more food rationing – and the sweet jars in Warman's corner shop would be full again – and there'd be ha'penny cornets . . . and perhaps, now Dad was learning to drive, they'd be able to go to the fair in Barry – or down Porthcawl, even.

It was going to be boring now all the excitement was over. What could she do? I know, I'll write it all down and send it to Abbie. Perhaps those neighbours that took them in would know her address. She'll be surprised at how it all turned out – and I could put it in our form magazine – that'll give it a good start. The others will never believe it, though. I expect they'll try to outdo me.

She went to find some paper and a pencil . . .

Details of the real Hans Kuhnemann

With acknowledgements to Dennis Morgan, *Cardiff, City at War*, John O'Sullivan, *A Century of Cardiff*, and Bill Barrett, 'My Cardiff', *Cardiff Post*.

Hans Kuhnemann was the managing director of The Flottmann Drill Company in Allensbank Road. He was a Nazi spy who sent information back to Germany up until the beginning of the war.

He was a former Prussian Guards Officer and looked the part, being very tall, arrogant and sporting a monocle. He made no secret of his affiliation to Germany (his office was decorated with photographs of Hitler and Ribbentrop) and he and sympathizers frequently held Anglo-German nights in the Park Hotel, Cardiff where they would drink Hitler's health and smash the glasses in the fireplace. They very soon had to move to a new venue when the manager protested about their behaviour.

He used to travel through the Midlands and South Wales gleaning information about military and industrial establishments and taking photographs – some from the air on pleasure trips from Pengam Airport. The Special Branch were aware of his activities and at the outbreak of the war on 3rd September they went to his house in Marlborough Road, only to find that he had left Cardiff and gone to the German Embassy where he helped destroy documents.

He then escaped back to Germany where his photographs and information were collated into aerial guide books for the Luftwaffe and provided invaluable information for their bombers.

The 'Mr Brown' in my story is an entirely fictitious character. He is meant to be a 'sleeper', someone planted by the enemy from an early age so that he will have a British background and not be a suspect in the event of war.

These are the organisations which are often
mentioned in the story:

WJAC   Women's Junior Air Corps
ATC   Air Training Corps
WAAF   Women's Auxiliary Air Force
RAF   Royal Air Force